Plundered Treasure

PLUNDERED TREASURE

Charlotte Carter

Guideposts

NEW YORK, NEW YORK

Knock-knock jokes: www.ahajokes.com and www.knock-knock-joke.com
Original jokes by Charlotte Lobb

www.guideposts.com
(800) 431-2344
Guideposts Books & Inspirational Media

Cover and interior design by Cindy LaBreacht
Cover art by Gail W. Guth
Map by Jim Haynes, represented by Creative Freelancers, Inc.
Typeset by Nancy Tardi
Printed in the United States of America

ORCAS

To
U.S.A.

LUMMI

N
W E
S

CYPRESS

GUEMES

To
ANACORTES

FIDALGO
ISLAND

*SPARROW ISLAND IS FICTITIOUS

CHAPTER 🌹 ONE

A THICK BLANKET OF GRAY clouds blocked the sun, turning late afternoon in the San Juan Islands in Washington State into an early twilight. Fine mist dampened streets and decorated shrubs with shimmering raindrops. Eaves dripped in a drowsy rhythm as the islanders waited impatiently for true spring to arrive.

On Sparrow Island, the shrill ring of the phone woke Mary Reynolds from her nap. Her eyes blinked open.

For a moment, she was disoriented, thinking she had slept the night away. But her bedside clock read 4:36 PM as the phone jangled again.

She yawned. "Goodness, I certainly must have needed that nap. I was dead to the world. Now it's almost time to start dinner."

As though responding to Mary's comment, Finnegan, her Labrador/golden retriever service dog, rose from his spot on the floor next to the bed and stretched.

The insistent ringing continued. Mary reached for the phone and then remembered she had left it on the coffee table in the living room.

No need to rush, Mary thought.

With the help of a trapeze bar, she eased from the bed into her wheelchair. Since the car accident that had left her paralyzed from the waist down, she'd learned to live life not at a sprint but at a slower pace. Whoever was calling would either leave a message on the answering machine or call her on her cell phone, which she kept tucked in a denim bag tied to her wheelchair.

The phone grew silent. Finally.

Chances were good that the caller was a telemarketer anyway. Most of her friends knew to call her cell number.

In the bathroom, she splashed water on her face and added a touch of gloss to her lips. She ran a comb through her hair, which had long ago turned silver. But still, as a fifty-eight-year-old, she didn't look bad.

As she wheeled toward the living room, she heard Finnegan growling.

He barked furiously and raced ahead of her, as she heard something shatter.

"What on earth!" Had Blossom, her cat, knocked over something? "Be careful, Finnegan. Come back!"

She caught up with the dog in time to see the figure of a man fleeing out the open sliding glass door. Her lamp on the floor in pieces provided all the evidence she needed.

A stranger had broken into her house!

"Dear Lord!" She grabbed Finnegan's ruff to restrain him from chasing after the man. "Quiet, boy! Sit!"

A gust of wind blew in the open door. She shivered. Had the stranger intended to rob her? Or worse?

With a shaking hand, she fumbled for her cell phone, flipped it open and punched the speed dial for Sgt. Henry Cobb.

Please, Lord, let him be here on Sparrow Island. As the sergeant in charge of the local sheriff's substation, Henry had to cover not only Sparrow Island, but Lopez and Shaw Islands as well.

He answered on the second ring. "Hi, Mary," he said with a warm smile in his voice. "What's up?"

"I—" Her voice cracked, tears pressed at the back of her eyes. "I just had a break-in. A man—"

"Where are you?" His tone changed completely. Concerned. Professional. "At Island Blooms?"

"No, I'm not at the flower shop. I'm at home."

"Is the intruder still in the house?"

"No. He ran off."

"Okay. Lock yourself in. I'm on my way. Five minutes, Mary."

The siren on his patrol car screamed in Mary's ear, and she knew he'd been running to the car as he spoke.

"I'll be there in five minutes," he told her again.

Thank God! she thought.

She rolled over to the door and then realized she couldn't do much since the lock appeared to be broken. The stranger had reached right in and . . .

Hastily wheeling back away from the door, she looked around the room, everything so familiar but now somehow different. Abby's Bible sitting on the small table was strangely jarring, juxtaposed in her mind's eye with the man who had violated her home. Fear formed a knot in Mary's stomach. The interloper had shattered not only her lamp, but her sense of security as well.

What if he came back?

She moved to the kitchen, grabbed a carving knife and wheeled around again, brandishing the bone-handled weapon in her hand.

She felt her panic rising again. *Please, Lord, help me to stay calm and do whatever has to be done.*

Finnegan whined.

"It's all right, boy. Henry will be here soon." Henry was more than just a deputy sheriff. He was her beau. He cared for her and she cared deeply about him.

She heard the approaching siren.

Still agitated, Finnegan barked and took an aggressive posture, his legs braced.

"Come on. Let's go let Henry in." She rolled her chair to the front door. When she opened it, she saw the car parked cattywampus in front of the house and Henry running up the walkway.

"Thank goodness you got here so quickly."

"Are you all right?"

"I'm fine." Tears threatened again, and her chin trembled. "I was so scared. . . ."

He knelt in front of her chair. His weathered, age-lined face and the fringe of gray hair on his head were dear to her, and the obvious concern in his brown eyes brought a lump to her throat. He'd come to her aid in such a rush that he hadn't bothered to straighten his green uniform tie, the knot loose at his open shirt collar. He wasn't even wearing his Smokey-the-Bear campaign hat.

He was simply there with her.

"How 'bout you give me the knife before you accidentally

stick me with it." Gently, he took the knife she'd forgotten she had from her hand. Then he wrapped his strong arms around her and held her tight. "You weren't the only one who was scared," he whispered.

"I wanted to go after that man, ring his neck myself," she said. "But I couldn't, and I was afraid to let Finnegan chase him down for fear my valiant dog would be hurt."

"You did the right thing, calling me."

Smiling faintly, she rested her head on Henry's shoulder. The rapid beating of her heart finally began to slow.

AS ABBY STANTON LEFT the Nature Museum, she looked up at the overcast sky. She'd spent most of the day inside at her desk entering data from the recent bald eagle count on Sparrow Island into her computer. She was ready for some sunshine. But it was not to be this afternoon.

And with Friday drawing to an end, the weather report didn't promise much better for the weekend.

Normally, Abby's job as the nature conservatory's Associate Curator allowed her to be outdoors much of her workweek, which was one of the reasons she'd accepted the position. There were days like this one, however, that kept her cooped up with paperwork.

Of course, the biggest reason she'd left her longtime job at Cornell University's Lab of Ornithology and returned to Sparrow Island was to help her sister Mary after her accident. What a blessing that decision had become. Not only had she and Mary put the squabbles of childhood behind them, they'd become great friends as well as roommates. Living together in the home where Mary had raised her family was an arrangement that suited them both. And being near her parents, who were both in their eighties, allowed Abby to check on them regularly. Something she had missed while living in New York.

In the nearly empty parking lot, she slid into her hybrid car for the short drive home through the quiet town of Green Harbor. No long commutes for her, a definite plus with any job.

She took a moment to clean her glasses hoping the day would appear a little brighter. That failing, she turned on the headlights against the gloom and backed out of the parking space.

The shops in town were still open, but there were few pedestrians going about their business. Summer would see a much more animated community.

As she approached home—a light blue, two-story house in a residential area—Abby spotted Henry Cobb's police cruiser parked crazily on the wrong side of the street, the flashing lights still swirling, the driver's door standing open. Her heart leapt into her throat. Could something have happened to Mary?

She whipped the car into the driveway and was out almost before it came to a full stop. She ran to the front door and shoved it open.

"Mary!" she shouted.

"In the living room, dear."

Abby followed the sound of her sister's voice. "What's wrong?"

"Everything's all right," Henry said. "There was a break-in. Probably an attempted robbery. Finnegan frightened the robber off and Mary wasn't hurt."

"Oh my goodness!" Alarmed for her sister's well-being, Abby covered her mouth with her hand. With a quick scan of the living room, she noted the broken lamp and Finnegan standing next to Mary, clearly being extra-protective of his mistress. "Thank heaven for Finnegan."

"Yes." Mary dropped her hand to the dog's head and petted him. "He was very brave."

In response to Mary's praise, Finnegan wagged his tail.

"Did you get a look at whoever broke in?" Abby asked.

"Not a very good one, I'm afraid. I was just telling Henry. It all happened so fast, and I only saw him from the back as he ran out the door. I'm sure it was a man, no one I recognized. He was wearing a dark shirt or jacket—I can't even be sure whether it was black or navy blue—and a matching baseball cap."

"Not much to go on, is it?" Abby commented, shaking her head. Half the men on Sparrow Island probably owned a dark jacket or shirt, and they all had baseball caps of one kind or another.

"You said he had on work boots," Henry reminded her.

"Oh, yes. The sort of heavy boots men who do construction work usually wear."

"That doesn't narrow the field a whole lot," Abby said.

"I've got a deputy on the way over to check for fingerprints," Henry said. "I'm not optimistic though. These guys are usually smart enough to wear gloves."

A chill breeze caught the vertical blinds, swaying them.

"After your deputy checks for fingerprints, maybe we can get Aaron Holloway from the hardware store over here to replace the lock." The cold air cut through Abby's denim jacket and she wrapped her arms around herself.

"Good idea," Henry agreed.

"Anyone here?" came a shout from the front door.

Henry grimaced. "That's gotta be William Jansen from the *Birdcall*. He drives me crazy, listening to the police frequency, showing up at every crime scene looking for a story."

Abby half smiled to herself. "I think he's hoping to win a Pulitzer some day for his reporting." That he had spent most of his adult life working for his family's diaper manufacturing business in Chicago before pursuing his dream of journalism continued to amaze and amuse Abby.

She stepped into the dining room. "We're in here, William."

The owner of the *Birdcall* came storming in, his slender physique all but shrouded in a brown suit that matched the nondescript color of his thinning hair, bushy eyebrows and mustache.

"I heard Mary had a break-in. What was taken? Was she hurt?" He was already scribbling notes on the pad he always carried in his pocket.

"Nothing was taken and Mary's fine. Come see for yourself."

In full reporter mode, he blustered his way past Abby.

"Easy, William," Henry warned. "This is a crime scene. I don't want you disturbing the evidence."

"Wouldn't think of it, Sergeant." He turned his attention to Mary. "Were you home when the break-in happened?"

"I was napping. The phone rang and woke me up. A few minutes later, Finnegan growled and then I heard the sound of the lamp breaking and I came in here. Finnegan chased the thief off, so I only got a quick glance at the man's back."

"It'll all be in my report," Henry said.

"Right." William jotted down another note. "You figure this break-in's related to the other robberies we've had, Henry?"

"What robberies?" Abby asked, surprised.

William scowled at her. "We've had four houses broken into in the past couple of weeks. Didn't you read about the break-ins in the *Birdcall*? Had a big headline this week. Story above the fold."

"I don't think we got a paper this week," Mary said, looking as surprised as Abby.

"Whaddaya mean, no paper? Every Wednesday, rain or shine, we publish the *Birdcall*."

"Can you folks take this conversation into the other room?" Henry requested.

"I went outside to look for the paper Wednesday morning," Abby recalled. "It wasn't there." She shrugged.

"Well, you should've called the office." Flipping to a new page in his notepad, William scribbled a reminder to himself. "I'll talk to my delivery man. Can't have him skipping houses."

"The other room, folks." Shooing them with his hands, Henry finally got them to move. "My deputy's here to check for fingerprints. Let's give him some space."

Right on cue, Deputy Mike Bennett appeared outside the back door carrying an evidence kit. He touched his fingertips to the brim of his cap in an informal salute.

"Hiya, Sarge," he said.

"I'll get these people out of your hair so you can get to work."

Abby walked to the far end of the living room. William and Mary followed, as did Finnegan. Before Abby had a chance to sit down, Sandy McDonald, their neighbor and friend, knocked on the open front door.

"What's going on?" she called. "I just got home from work and there're two police cars—"

"Come on in," Abby said, noticing that ten-year-old Bobby was with his mother. "We had a break-in."

Sandy's reaction, as Mary told the story again, was much the same as Abby's had been: surprise, shock and concern for Mary's safety.

While Sandy listened, she unbuttoned her jacket, revealing the sweater and pleated skirt she'd worn for her day of teaching at Green Harbor Public School. "I'm so glad you weren't hurt, Mary," she said when Mary had told her what had happened.

"I'm fine, thanks. Did you know there've been some other robberies lately in Green Harbor?"

"Margaret Blackstock was talking about it at school the other day," Sandy said. "That's the first I'd heard about any break-ins."

"You must have read the story in the *Birdcall*," William insisted.

Sandy looked puzzled. "You know, I think it's been a couple of weeks since we got the *Birdcall*."

"Well, there's certainly something wrong if neither of you are getting the paper," William groused. "But don't worry. I'll take care of it. Lynell Cowan will hear about this. I make it a point not to pay people who aren't doing their job."

"I'm sure it was just an oversight," Abby quickly offered, worried that the older gentleman who delivered the paper might be fired. She was sure he used the income to supplement his social security benefits. "You know, now that I think about it, one of the volunteers at the Nature Museum said something about a robbery in town. I was busy and didn't pay much attention."

William grumbled something under his breath. "If you've

been missing the paper, then you probably didn't see the photo of your father picketing the Senior Center. Page three in this week's issue, right up top."

Both Mary and Abby's heads snapped around toward William.

"Dad's picketing the Senior Center?" Mary exclaimed.

"Why on earth is he doing that?" Abby wanted to know.

Bobby spoke up, his hazel eyes bright with laughter. "I heard about that at school. It's cool. Mr. Stanton and some other old guys are mad that they're not getting their free donuts anymore 'cause somebody said donuts have too much cholesterol. Me and my friends think if the old guys get their donuts back, then maybe we can picket to get the snack machine with potato chips and candy bars 'n' stuff back. They switched to apples and granola bars." He wrinkled his nose, showing his disapproval of healthy snacks.

Sandy slipped her arm around Bobby's shoulders. "I don't think that's a good idea, honey. Too much sugar's bad for you."

"It'd be better than those squishy apples with all the brown spots on them and worms."

Deciding to leave the great apple versus candy debate to others, Abby slipped back over to the door. She wished now that she'd paid closer attention to the volunteer who'd brought up the subject of the break-ins. Of course, everyone probably assumed she'd read the news in the paper.

"How's it going?" she asked Deputy Bennett. Black powder that was going to be a mess to clean up covered the door and the doorjamb.

The deputy glanced toward her. "I've got lots of prints, but I'm guessing they belong to you and Mary."

"Probably so." She turned to Henry. "Would you mind if I dropped by the office tomorrow to check out the police reports on the other robberies?"

"No problem," Henry said. "They're public record. But I'll tell you, we've been scratching our combined heads trying to get a lead on who's doing the robberies. So far we don't have a clue."

"Well, maybe a new set of eyes will help." Abby was sure the rash of robberies was probably the work of the man Mary had seen. Abby had always been good at solving puzzles. Maybe by studying the official reports, she'd find a puzzle piece or two that would fit together.

Today's attempted robbery had struck home and, with God's help, Abby intended to make sure the perpetrator was held to account for his crimes.

CHAPTER ❦ TWO

By THE TIME THE MESS HAD been cleaned up and Aaron Holloway had repaired the broken lock, it was well past dinnertime. After all the excitement, neither Abby nor Mary had much of an appetite, so Mary pulled out a container of homemade soup from the freezer to heat, got out some crackers and they sat down at the kitchen table to eat.

"In all the years I've lived in this house," Mary said, "this is the only time we've had a break-in."

"Let's hope it's the last." The chicken and noodle soup with healthy chunks of vegetables was the perfect antidote to a stressful experience. "What do you suppose the thief was after?"

"I can't imagine. I certainly don't keep a lot of cash around, and what little jewelry I own wouldn't bring much money at a pawn shop."

"I've got diamond stud earrings and a gold necklace. That's about it for expensive jewelry," Abby said. She wondered if there was something else in the house with an intrinsic value that a criminal would risk jail time for. She had a porcelain bird collection upstairs in her room and Mary owned a few small antiques and her late husband Jacob's scrimshaw collection, but none of that seemed worth taking. "Maybe it was just a random break-in, and he was looking for anything he could find."

"I, for one, hope he looks somewhere else next time."

"I hope Henry identifies the thief and locks him up before he has a chance to strike again."

"Even better," Mary agreed.

Outside the window, clouds hid the night sky, leaving the glass to reflect the overhead kitchen light. The neighborhood was eerily hushed. No traffic noise. No car doors slamming shut, no one shouting a friendly greeting. After the break-in, everyone had locked their doors and was staying safely inside.

Their peaceful community no longer felt so serene and secure.

Thoughtfully, Abby finished her soup and munched on one last cracker. "Did I hear you say you had a phone call shortly before the break-in?"

"Yes, the phone woke me from my nap. I'd foolishly stayed up late last night trying to finish knitting a sweater for my Warm up America project, which meant I felt tired all day."

"Who was it that called?"

Mary glanced toward the phone. "You know, in all the excitement, I forgot to check the answering machine." She rolled herself the few feet to the phone to check. "Looks like whoever it was didn't leave a message, and they didn't call me on my cell, so it couldn't have been important."

"Does caller ID show the number?"

Mary shook her head. "The little screen says 'Unknown.'"

Evidently the caller had hung up before the phone switched to the answering machine. "Maybe they'll call back tomorrow."

"I'll be here. In fact, I think I'll stick close to home for a few days." Picking up her soup bowl, Mary carried it to the counter, which had been lowered to a convenient wheelchair height following her accident. Abby had overseen a complete remodel of the downstairs to make it accessible for Mary.

A ripple of anxiety shot down Abby's spine. She didn't like the idea of Mary's being here alone, not with a robber on the loose. A determined thief could easily get into the house despite the new lock Aaron had put on the back door. But there was no possible way Abby could stay home every day. In fact, Mary's schedule was generally as busy as her own since she divided her time between the flower shop and her numerous community activities.

She'd simply have to pray that the Lord would watch over Mary and keep her safe.

SATURDAY MORNING DAWNED with the sky as leaden as the previous day.

Bundling up in a warm sweatshirt and jacket, Abby took her book of daily devotions downstairs, poured herself a cup of coffee and stepped out onto the back deck. The ocean beyond Mary's backyard was the same flat pewter gray as the sky, the horizon nearly indistinguishable. The faint sound of waves lapping against the rocky shore drifted up to her.

Using an old towel, she wiped the dew from one of the two wicker chairs on the deck and sat down. Drawing in a deep breath of salt-tinged air, she opened her book.

The day's lesson was a timely one. "He who has been stealing must steal no longer, but must work, doing something useful with his own hands, that he may have something to share with those in need" (Ephesians 4:28).

As Abby read the rest of the lesson, she wondered if the Sparrow Island thief, a man who wore heavy boots, could be an unemployed workman desperate to feed his family or if his motivation was simply greed. Granted, jobs were hard to come by on the island during the off season. When the weather improved and summer tourists arrived, more opportunities to work were available.

From the corner of her eye, she noticed Blossom's stealthy approach through the tall grass. The white Persian cat stalked a hapless moth whose wings were not yet dry after the damp night. Blossom watched the moth's efforts to fly with studied interest but didn't pounce. Only when the moth took flight did the cat give chase. Unsuccessfully, in this case.

Smiling, Abby closed her book and bowed her head. Whatever the thief's motives, she prayed he would steal no longer and find his way to redemption.

SHORTLY AFTER NINE O'CLOCK, Abby arrived at the sheriff's substation on Municipal Street across from Green Harbor Public School. With little traffic and the school closed for the weekend, she angled into an empty parking spot right next to one of the silvery-tan police cruisers.

Inside, she found Deputy Artie Washburn on duty behind the counter. A Native American in his late twenties with burnished good looks, he wore his uniform with military precision.

"Good morning, Dr. Stanton." On the desk behind Artie

stood a small, hand-carved totem pole with the figure of an eagle on top. With each passing year, he became more skilled at the craft his ancestors had passed down to him. "Sorry to hear you had a break-in yesterday."

"I understand there's been a lot of that going around recently."

"Yes, ma'am. But we'll catch the guy soon. It's a small island, you know. Sooner or later, he'll mess up or brag to some buddy about what he's doing. Then we'll nail him good. You can count on that."

Abby certainly hoped Artie was right. "Henry said it'd be all right if I took a look at the crime reports of the previous house break-ins."

"Sure thing." He walked to a bank of steel filing cabinets against the back wall and slid open a drawer. A large photo of the Washington State governor hung above the cabinets. Below that were crossed American and state flags.

Plucking some forms from the file drawer, Artie returned to the counter. "You'll have to read these here. If you want to take them with you, I'll make copies for you."

"I'll take a look here first. I may have some questions."

Checking the dates, she put the forms in chronological order. The first robbery had taken place two weeks ago on a Tuesday at the home of Gary and Belinda Brisbin, who lived near Cedar Grove Lake. Some cash had been taken, estimated at less than a hundred dollars, as well as a laptop computer belonging to the Brisbins' daughter, Summer. Apparently no one had been home at the time of the break-in. Belinda reported the incident after she came home from work.

Abby glanced up from the report. "This must be Belinda who works at Beach Bag Books on Shoreline Drive?"

"Yes, ma'am. We hadn't had a break-in on Sparrow Island since last summer until the Brisbin case. Real shame. The Brisbins had some hard times lately and were just getting back on their feet and then, bingo! Life hits 'em hard again. The girl, Summer, needed that computer for her school work."

Abby vaguely recalled that Belinda had had a serious illness not too long ago and the daughter had dropped out of college for a time.

Turning that police report facedown on the counter, Abby turned her attention to the break-in that apparently occurred the same week. Brenda and Kyle Wilson, owners of the Tackle Shop, had been off-island to see their college-aged son. When they returned, they found the house had been broken into, several hundred dollars stolen, two PCs, a valuable antique fishing rod and an ancient Salish Indian wooden mask of a legendary woman who, it was said, lived under the water and cared for the plants and fish.

Brenda, a devoted fisher herself, must have highly prized that mask. What a shame someone had stolen it, a much more difficult possession to replace than cash or computers.

The remaining reports told a similar story. Opal Collins had been robbed of cash and some silver serving pieces that had been in her family for years. It appeared that Margaret Blackstock, the school secretary, had lost the most, including cash, silverware, two computers, a painting by a well-known artist in New York and a handcrafted Tlingit Indian rattle-top basket valued at twelve hundred dollars.

Goodness, the thief had found a regular gold mine here on Sparrow Island.

"Artie, if you don't mind, I think I would like copies of these reports."

"Sure thing, Dr. Stanton." He'd been working at his desk. Now he pushed his chair back and got the reports from her.

Within minutes, Abby had the copies she needed and was on her way to the Tackle Shop. Unless Brenda Wilson had a charter fishing trip this morning, she'd be at the store.

Police reports provided only the bare bones of the crime. Details could inadvertently be left out of the report. Or once the trauma had passed, victims sometimes recalled additional details they'd failed to mention in the initial police interview.

Abby hoped to glean new information by talking with the victims directly.

Located on Kingfisher Street, the Tackle Shop was only a block from the sheriff's substation, so Abby decided to walk the short distance. The moisture in the air made the temperature feel much cooler than it was, probably in the midfifties. She zipped up her jacket and set a quick pace.

Stores were beginning to open now, and there was more traffic on the streets. But without the surge of tourists the island would see later in the year, the town felt cozy and friendly. People waved. Drivers tooted their horns in greeting as friends passed by.

Surely if there were a thief in their midst, he would be a stranger and an unfamiliar face among the locals.

Most of the shops along the street had green awnings that were extended over the sidewalk when it was raining and on hot summer days for shade. But on such an overcast day, the awnings were all retracted so as much light as possible could seep in through the display windows. Abby pushed open the glass door to the Tackle Shop, located in a quaint building that was probably a hundred years old. A bell tinkled to announce her arrival.

Sitting at a desk, Brenda was bent over looking through a high-powered magnifying glass while she tied a fishing fly. An assortment of feathers, threads and hooks were on the table beside her.

"I'll be right with you," she said without looking up.

"No hurry," Abby responded. She glanced around the shop intrigued at the array of bamboo and fiberglass fishing rods on the wall and shelves full of spinning reels and tackle boxes in a half-dozen colors and sizes. She remembered going fishing with her father, who'd once owned his own charter boat, but she'd forgotten how many kinds of rods were available; different styles for salt water, fresh water, fly fishing or bait casting. She wondered how Brenda kept them all straight.

Brenda finished the fly and stood, rotating her head to ease the tension from her neck. Even in winter, her blonde hair was sun-streaked and her face tanned from the hours she spent outdoors.

"Hey, Abby. You want to book a charter? I know just where to find us a big ol' king salmon for supper."

Abby laughed. "Not today, I'm afraid."

"Too bad. So what can I do for you?" She adjusted the khaki fishing vest she perpetually wore and strolled over to the counter.

Abby told her about the break-in at Mary's and how she was investigating the prior robberies to see if she could come up with a suspect.

"Sorry to hear about Mary's house being hit, though I'm glad she was able to run the thief off." Brenda straightened a pile of fishing regulation booklets on the counter. "I tell you, it was a real shock for me 'n' Kyle to come home from visiting our son at college and find a window broken, our PCs gone and whatever cash we had in the house missing. Plus, the jerk took my grandfather's handmade bamboo rod right off the wall. Now why'd he have to do that? It can't be worth much."

"I imagine the Salish water woman's mask that was taken was worth more," Abby said.

Brenda shrugged. "Certainly it had sentimental value. Kyle bought that for me years ago at the Salish reservation on the mainland. Some festival they were having. He always said I was his own personal water woman." A blush deepened the color of her tanned cheeks.

"That was sweet of him."

"Yeah, he's all right. I'm lucky he puts up with me."

Most people thought that the Tackle Shop belonged to Kyle. But the truth was that Brenda ran the fishing end of the business and Kyle took care of the paperwork, rarely dropping a line in the water. The arrangement seemed to work fine for the couple.

"Since you filed the police report, have you discovered anything else missing or out of place? Maybe drawers that were rifled? Or a coin collection, stamps, something you don't bring out to look at regularly is now gone?"

"I don't think so. The thief was pretty neat and tidy about the whole thing and we're not much for collecting anything except fishing lures. I've got some that are collectibles. The deputy who checked for fingerprints left kind of a mess though. Kyle had to clean it up."

Abby could relate to that. "If you think of anything else, anything at all, let me know. And Sergeant Cobb, of course."

"Sure. I just hope the guy's caught before somebody gets hurt."

⁴ "I do too." That was of particular concern for Abby since the thief had failed to get whatever he came for at Mary's house. He could decide to try again.

Taking a chance that Belinda Brisbin was working at Beach Bag Books this morning, Abby strolled down toward the waterfront where the store was located. A ferry had just arrived from Friday Harbor, and a line of cars bumped their way up the ramp to the road. Probably there were a few tourists on board, but she imagined most of passengers lived here or elsewhere in the San Juan Islands.

Belinda was a devoted fan of romance novels, so it was no surprise to find her sitting on a stool behind the cash register, reading a paperback when there were no customers in the shop.

"Is it a good one?" Abby asked.

Glancing up, Belinda grinned, then checked the cover of the book as though to remind herself what book she was reading. "One of my favorite authors. I highly recommend her books, if you'd like to give one a try."

"Oh, you know me. I'm more into mystery novels than romance." In fact, she'd been reading mysteries since she'd gone through an entire set of Nancy Drew mysteries the summer she was nine years old.

"We just got a new shipment of best sellers in yesterday, including some new mysteries. Take a look." She gestured toward the front of the store and a table filled with hardcover books.

"Actually, I'm working on a real-life mystery at the moment."

Once again, Abby told how a would-be thief had broken into Mary's house and been run off by Finnegan.

"If we were home more, I'd be tempted to get a dog myself," Belinda said. "But it seems so unfair to have a pet and not be there to give it some attention. Dogs can get so lonely when they're left alone all day."

"That's true. What I'm wondering is if you've thought of any new details about what happened at your house or what was stolen during the break-in."

Frowning, Belinda took off her glasses and cleaned them with a cloth. "All I know is that I was scared senseless when I walked into the house and found that someone had broken my dining room window. And when I discovered the thief had taken the money I'd saved for my daughter's birthday, I was madder than hops. I don't know about you, but extra money doesn't grow on trees around our house."

"Let's hope when they catch the man, he'll be able to make restitution."

Belinda's laugh sounded bitter. "That sounds like more of a fantasy than these books I love to read." She held up the paperback in her hand.

Abby sympathized with the middle-aged woman and counted her blessings that she had her health and her financial situation was comfortable. Not everyone was that fortunate.

"Well, if anything about the robbery occurs to you that you haven't already mentioned to the sheriff's deputies, let me know. There's no such thing as a perfect crime. All it takes is one little clue or a tiny mistake on the part of the thief, and Henry Cobb will be able to track him down."

But so far, Abby hadn't been able to find that telling clue and neither had Henry.

All in God's time, she reminded herself.

CHAPTER ❦ THREE

A KNOCK ON THE BACK door startled Mary. Her breath caught in her throat.

Her first thought was that the robber had come back to try his luck again. But Finnegan looked expectantly toward the back door, his tail wagging. The visitor must be a friend, she realized with relief. *Don't be such a nervous Nellie*, she coached herself, *especially since a thief wouldn't knock.*

Putting the skein of variegated yarn she was balling in her lap, she wheeled to the door. She spotted Bobby McDonald, his baseball cap tipped back on his head, grinning at her. Smart as a firecracker, he was welcome on this cloudy morning.

"Good morning, young man," she said as she opened the door. "Hope you're here to help me ball up my yarn. I'm getting ready to start another sweater."

"Sure, I can do that. But first Mom wanted me to check to see how're you're feeling today."

She rolled back from the door to let him in. "You can tell her I'm fine, thank you."

"Yesterday must have been pretty scary."

"It was," she admitted, wheeling to the kitchen. "But no real harm done, thank the good Lord."

Bobby petted Finnegan and scratched him under his chin. "Mom also said I should ask if you were busy before I asked you to help me with something."

"Oh? What's that?"

He dropped a spiral notebook and the stub of a pencil on the table so he could use both hands to scratch both of Finnegan's jowls. "I'm going to enter a contest and I need somebody to help me write some jokes."

Mary did a mental double take. "You want me to write jokes for you?" She was good at knitting and sewing, even scrapbooking, but she'd never written anything in her life other than letters to friends and family.

"Yeah, haven't you heard?" He plopped down in one of the kitchen chairs, and Finnegan rested his muzzle on the boy's thigh, delighted with Bobby's attention. "Springhouse Café is having an open mic night for standup comics, two weeks from next Thursday. Whoever tells the best jokes 'n' stuff wins four free tickets to their first Sunday brunch of the season next month."

"That's quite a prize." Starting in April every year, the café offered a popular Sunday brunch with enough food to lure every tourist in the entire state of Washington, as well as all the locals on Sparrow Island, into the restaurant.

"I want to win so I can take Mom and Dad to breakfast and they won't have to pay anything."

"I see."

"I'll get an extra ticket if I win, so I can take you, too, if you'll help me."

"Providing me with an incentive, huh?" She suppressed a smile. "That's very generous of you. But I'm afraid I don't know how to write a joke." Being a standup comedienne hadn't been one of her life goals. In fact, speaking to a group wasn't one of her favorite things to do. As a child, she'd practically broken out in hives when she had to give a speech at school. One time when she was singing a solo for a high school event, she'd been so plagued by stage fright, she'd forgotten the words to the song.

No, she had no intention of performing for a crowd again.

"That's okay." He flipped open his notebook. "I looked up some stuff in books at the library. You know, about how to write jokes. But I'm having a hard time coming up with the punch lines."

"And you want me to help you?" She was sure they'd both be better off if she stuck to her knitting.

"Yeah. Everybody says you have a great sense of humor."

"They do?"

"Sure." He applied the worn-down tip of his pencil to his notepaper. "First thing we have to do is decide what kind of stuff I can talk about. You know, real things like being ten years old, going to school, going fishing. Stuff like that."

Stuff Mary could barely remember being or doing. "Then what?"

"Then you figure out what's *weird* about being ten or fishing or going to school. See, it's all about attitude."

Mary picked up the ball of yarn she was winding. Frankly, she thought it was weird the yarn manufacturer didn't sell it wound into a ball in the first place. Surely they had a machine that could do it faster than she could.

"So what do you think is weird about being ten?" she prompted.

"I dunno. That's the problem." His lips twisted into a crooked smile. "That's how come I came over here to see you."

"Couldn't your mother help you?"

He gazed at her intently, his hazel eyes serious. "I love my mom a whole lot, but I don't think she's funny. Do you?"

Mary choked on a laugh. Sandy McDonald was a lovely lady and had a fine sense of humor. But maybe her own offspring couldn't see that.

"All right, let me see if I can remember what it's like being ten." Her hands worked the yarn instinctively as she gave the subject some thought. "You're too short to reach the top shelf. You can't drive a car. You get called a baby if you cry, but you're not allowed to do grownup things yet."

"These are great, Mary." He furiously wrote down her ideas.

"Let's see . . . When you're ten, the girls are interested in boys, but the boys aren't interested in them."

"That's not *weird*, Mary. That's *scary!*"

She chuckled.

"Last week a whole bunch of girls chased me around the school yard trying to kiss me."

"Oh dear."

"I had to hide out in the boy's restroom the whole recess period. But what's really scary is that by the time I'm sixteen, Dad says I'll stop running and *want* to kiss them." He shuddered dramatically and waggled his tongue in distaste.

Mary laughed out loud. "There's your joke, Bobby. It's perfect!"

"Really?" His eyes widened in surprise.

"I laughed, didn't I? Write it down. And when you tell the joke, be sure to act out how you feel about kissing girls."

"Yeah, it's gross." Not entirely convinced they'd created a winner, he scribbled the joke in his notebook.

Just then the phone rang.

"Want me to answer it for you?"

"If you'd like."

He picked up on the second ring. "Reynolds residence," he said. "Bobby McDonald—" He looked at Mary. "They hung up."

"Oh well. It was probably a telemarketer anyway."

Bobby cradled the phone. "My mom gets really upset when telemarketers call during dinner. And it's the worst just before an election. Somebody's always calling wanting her to vote for a candidate or something."

Mary admitted those computer-dialed calls annoyed her too.

Getting back to the business at hand, they continued to work on creating more jokes. By the time they ran out of steam and ideas, Mary had balled the entire skein of yarn and Abby had returned home for lunch. She strolled into the kitchen and greeted them.

"Did you find out anything interesting from the crime reports?" Mary asked.

"Not so far." Taking off her jacket, Abby draped it over the back of a kitchen chair. "I've talked to two of the victims, but they didn't have much to add to the report. I'll run out to see Opal Collins this afternoon and try to see Margaret Blackstock too."

"Margaret was robbed?" Mary asked.

"Yes, and had some valuable items taken too."

Bobby chimed in. "Everybody at school was talking about that the other day. Guess she was really upset. She took the afternoon off to go talk to some insurance guy."

At the stove, Abby put some water on to heat for tea. "I imagine having a break-in is like having a car accident. Even if you're not badly hurt, you still have to fuss with your insurance to cover the repair bills."

"Poor Margaret," Mary said. "And poor Opal too." Opal was in Mary's knitting group and made beautiful scarves. A single lady in her seventies, she lived alone and must have been terrified to discover her house had been robbed. That sort of thing simply didn't happen on Sparrow Island. Usually.

Abby leaned back against the counter, waiting for the water to boil. "So what have you two been up to this morning?"

"We've been writing jokes for open mic night at the Springhouse Café," Bobby said.

Abby's eyebrows drew together. "You're what?"

Bobby explained about the contest, then told her his joke about the girls chasing him into the bathroom at school.

Laughing, Abby said, "That's good, Bobby. Very funny."

"Mary helped me a lot. In fact, I think she ought to write some jokes for herself and enter the contest."

"Oh no. Not me." She shook her head. "No way am I going to get up in front of a crowd and tell jokes. I'd be too nervous."

"You'd be great," Bobby insisted. "You could tell a joke about how it's weird to be in a wheelchair all the time."

"I don't think there's a whole lot that's funny about being in a wheelchair."

"You can make it funny." Bobby spoke with such confidence, Mary was tempted to try.

"What's really weird is what businesses think makes a place accessible. I've been to restaurants that I had to enter through the kitchen. But I figured out how to handle that. I just pick up the next order that's ready and deliver it to the waiting customer." Mary winked at the boy. "Got a ten dollar tip once."

"You didn't!" Abby gasped on a laugh.

Bobby's eyes were wide with disbelief and twinkling with laughter.

"Bobby's right," Abby said. "You've got to enter that contest. You're a natural."

Mary disagreed. It was one thing to come up with an impromptu joke. But performing a whole routine in front of strangers? No, that wasn't her cup of tea.

DRIVING TO OPAL COLLINS' HOME took Abby on the road past the Sparrow Island Nature Conservatory and the old-growth forest that formed a part of the conservatory grounds. New grass had sprung up along the side of the road, disguising the brown winter-killed grass with a new coat of bright green—a sure sign that spring would show up on the island soon.

Opal's house was a small, two-story, shingled structure with a huge Pacific madrone tree near the road, easily identifiable by its reddish bark. Mature fir trees formed a horseshoe around the house itself, hiding it from the neighbor's view. Abby had to wonder how a would-be thief would know to target such a modest home when there were far more expensive residences on the island.

She parked the car and walked up onto the porch. A large black cat dozing in a wicker chair stared at her with unblinking yellow eyes. Abby rang the bell, and a moment later Opal answered the door.

"Well, isn't this a nice surprise." Wearing a simple dress and a hand-knitted cardigan sweater, Opal opened the door wider. "Do come in, Abby. I'll put some water on for tea."

"Oh, please don't bother. I don't plan to stay long." Abby stepped into a living room filled with overstuffed chairs and knickknacks covering every horizontal surface. There was the scent of vanilla in the air, probably from the candle burning on the counter. "I just wanted to ask you a few questions about the break-in you experienced."

"What a terrible thing! I haven't been able to sleep nights since then, I'll tell you that. Why, I jump at every little noise now." She picked up the knitting she'd left on the seat of a wingback chair and gestured for Abby to take the matching chair catty-cornered from hers. A few strands of her gray hair had escaped her usually neat bouffant hairdo.

"I'm so sorry, Opal. Maybe you should ask a friend to stay with you for a few days."

"Mercy, I've been living alone so long, it doesn't seem right that I'd let some thief frighten me into getting a roommate. I'll get over it soon enough."

"You're a brave lady." When she sat down, Abby sank deeper into the chair cushion than she'd expected, the stuffing not as firm in such an old chair. "I've been following up on all the robberies we've had lately, and I was wondering if you've remembered anything new since you filed the police report. Anything else missing that you hadn't realized initially?"

"I don't think so. I'm just sick about losing my mother's silver tea and coffee service though. She was so proud of that. Her brother sent it to her when he was in France during the First World War. He later died of his wounds. Of course, my father was in the war, too, but he made it home unscathed."

Abby's heart went out to Opal's family. How hard it must have been to lose a son.

"Before your break-in did you happen to notice any strangers in the neighborhood?" Abby asked.

"You mean, someone casing the place and planning to rob me?"

"Something like that. Maybe a workman?"

"Well, let me think." She picked up her needles and started on a new row of what appeared to be a scarf. "There was a crew resurfacing the street down the road. But they didn't get this far. I wish they had, though. Every winter we get more potholes in the street, and some of them are big enough to swallow a car, if you ask me. Course, the potholes slow the traffic down some, which is a help. Kids drive too fast these days, don't you think?"

"Sometimes that's true," Abby agreed. "Anyone else you can think of? Maybe a hiker passing through?"

"The school bus comes by every morning and afternoon. But that's been happening ever since I was a child. Course, this time of year I'm not outside much, so there's not much chance I'd see a stranger. My old bones don't like the cold, damp weather, don't you know."

Once again, Abby had hit a dead end. The Sparrow Island thief hadn't left her much of a trail to follow. Little wonder Henry hadn't come up with any leads so far.

To get to Margaret Blackstock's house, Abby had to go back through town. She decided she'd stop at the Green Grocer first to pick up some fresh produce for dinner, then go by Margaret's house on the way home.

While not a large grocery store, the Green Grocer carried virtually everything both tourists and locals might want. And if Archie Goodfellow, the owner, didn't have something you needed, he'd special order it from his suppliers.

Archie was working at the checkout counter when Abby walked in. A big man, who wore a royal-green butcher apron with a caricature of himself stenciled on the front, he towered over a group of children buying candy and ice cream bars. Apparently the children were determined to counter the healthy snacks at school with a binge of junk food on the weekend.

"All that sugar will rot your teeth," Archie muttered as he rang up the sale.

"I'll brush my teeth real good," the youngster promised, giggling.

"You better," his friend warned, "or your teeth will turn green and black and fall out."

"Yours too," the first boy countered, elbowing his buddy.

Selecting a grocery cart, Abby acknowledged Archie with a wave and made her way to the produce department. To her surprise, Margaret Blackstock was in the process of selecting a cantaloupe. She held one up and sniffed the stem.

"Are they ripe?" Abby asked.

Margaret started and looked up. "Not even close. I'd *kvetch* about it to Archie, but it wouldn't do any good." Even after living on Sparrow Island for more than ten years, her Brooklyn accent and an occasional phrase gave away her roots.

"It should ripen on the counter, don't you think?" Picking up a cantaloupe, Abby tested the stem end, which was green and hard to her touch. She put it back where she'd found it.

"Maybe in a week from Sunday." Margaret replaced the cantaloupe, picked up a honeydew from an adjacent bin and gave it a thump with her finger. On her day off as school secretary, her hairdo was in slight disarray and her lipstick had worn off. But she had on a neon orange blouse with a striped skirt that brightened a gray weekend.

"Ah, that's more like it," Margaret said. She slid the honeydew into her grocery cart.

"I'll take your word for it." Abby selected a melon to examine. "I'm glad I ran into you here. I was planning to drop by your house this afternoon."

"Oh? Whad'ya want?"

Abby set the melon down in her cart. "I wanted to talk to you about the robbery at your house."

"Oh, Abby! It's a terrible thing to have someone break into your home and take your precious things."

"Yes, I can imagine. I read the police report. You lost quite a lot."

"Tell me about it. That beautiful painting of Central Park that Joe gave me when we moved out here so I wouldn't get homesick. And the silverware I inherited from my mother. Plus, that Tlingit Indian basket was worth a fair piece of change too. Wilma Washburn attested to its authenticity, and she really knows her Native American crafts."

"Yes, I know." Wilma worked as the receptionist at the Nature Museum and had been instrumental in helping to create a display of Native American culture. "I'm following up on all the break-ins, hoping I can find some clue that Sergeant Cobb may have overlooked." Abby was quickly embarrassed by the comment, which sounded arrogant even to her own ears.

Henry and his small cadre of men always conducted a thorough investigation of any crime that happened here on the island. "I'm afraid these robberies have gotten personal. We had a break-in at our house, too, but Mary was there and scared the thief off."

"Mercy, what's our town coming to? I hope Mary's all right."

"The whole incident unsettled her. That's why I'm doing a little investigating on my own. I want that man caught before he tries again."

"I don't know how much I can help you," Margaret said. She moved around to the other side of the display to check out heads of lettuce.

"Well, for one, did you see any strangers around your house in the days before the break-in?"

"Not likely. On school days I'm gone from seven thirty in the morning 'til four-something in the afternoon."

"Has Joe said anything about seeing a stranger or anything odd or out of place in the neighborhood?"

Margaret selected a head of lettuce, dropped it in her cart, then picked up a cucumber. "I remember him mentioning one of the neighbors must have a phone problem 'cause a telephone company truck was parked down the street a ways. But you know how when we get a rainstorm the phone lines go down more times than not."

"True. It's almost as if the phone company isn't aware it rains in the San Juan Islands and doesn't prepare for that contingency."

Margaret laughed. "But really the worst part of the break-in, besides losing so much and having a broken window to deal with, was filling out all the insurance papers. You know, proving what the silverware and painting were worth. Then, on top of that, we have a pretty big deductible on our homeowners' insurance. So we've lost our things and a big chunk of change, too, if we try to replace what we've lost. If it was up to me, I'd string up the thief by his thumbs. If it turns out the culprits are some of my darling teenagers from school, I'll do worse than that."

Fortunately, Abby didn't think Margaret would actually take drastic action in either case. But she could empathize with the sentiment.

"Is there any particular reason you think teenagers might be behind the string of break-ins?" Abby asked. Mary hadn't described the would-be thief as an adolescent, but she hadn't gotten a close look at him.

"Oh, you know how some kids are. They get bored, make silly phone calls, like asking if your refrigerator's running, and when you say yes, they tell you you'd better go catch it."

Grimacing, Abby remembered a few college students who loved to pull pranks that were far more difficult to pull off than simply making crank phone calls. One group at Cornell had disassembled a professor's Model-T and reassembled it on top of the gym roof. The professor had quit his job at the end of the semester.

"Maybe our current crop of teenagers is getting more creative and greedy," Margaret concluded.

A thief did more than steal an individual's property, Abby reflected. He stole something of value from the entire community: a sense of safety.

Talking to the victims hadn't gotten Abby any closer to identifying the thief. She'd have to try a new approach. But, for now, she'd concentrate on selecting the fixings for a nice dinner salad. Tomorrow was a day of rest and worship, and time to be with her family.

On Monday, she'd start off fresh and prayed that God would set her footsteps in the right direction.

CHAPTER ❦ FOUR

I DON'T KNOW WHY WOMEN go to the expense and trouble of using Botox," Mary said. "I just let the fat fill in the wrinkles for me."

Abby burst out in laughter. They were en route to church on Sunday morning in Mary's specially equipped van, Finnegan secured behind the driver's seat where he could look out the windshield.

"You're not fat, Mary."

"I know. But I was just thinking . . ."

"Did you make up that joke with Bobby?" Abby asked. "It's very funny."

Mary shot her a glance. "That wasn't a joke. I was thinking about a doctor I saw on the morning show talking about plastic surgery and Botox. I simply think it's silly for a woman, or a man, for that matter, to worry about aging and getting a few wrinkles. They add character to a person's face. Besides, that's what God intended."

"But it's a great joke. You ought to put it in your routine."

Mary's jaw clenched. "I don't *have* a routine. And I'm not going to stand up in front of everyone at the Springhouse Café and make a fool of myself."

"But you're a natural." Mary's humor had always been on the dry side, largely because she wasn't trying to be funny. The humor came from who she was. Done with a straight face, her jokes would be hilarious.

Mary appeared uninterested in pursuing the conversation, so Abby dropped the subject. Still, it'd be a hoot to see Mary perform a comic routine.

"By the way," Abby said, "I asked the other break-in victims if they'd seen any workmen in their neighborhoods around the time of the robberies. Do you remember seeing any work going on around us?"

"Not offhand. None of the neighbors are doing any remodeling that I've noticed."

"No street workers? Anyone like that?"

"Not that I noticed. But then, I'm out of the house a lot at Island Blooms or at one of my meetings."

Abby had always been impressed with the number of activities Mary enjoyed and her involvement in the community. Becoming handicapped hadn't slowed her down one whit.

"Well, if you recall seeing anyone, let me know."

They joined a line of cars turning into Little Flock Church. A white picket fence covered with rhododendrons not yet in full bloom lined the driveway to the parking lot. The church itself was a tall, narrow building topped by a shingled steeple and a weathered metal cross. A sign out front indicated the church had been built in 1884, a part of the early history of the island.

Mary parked, then Abby climbed out of the passenger side of the van while Mary and Finnegan exited via a special lift. Taking the wheelchair handles, Abby pushed Mary toward the double-door entrance to the church. Finnegan trotted alongside Mary, his blue cape identifying him as a service dog. His harness allowed the dog to pull Mary if the going got tough.

Although the day was overcast, the clouds had lifted and watery sunlight struggled to break through the gray. Members of the congregation talked in animated groups of three or four, no doubt buoyed by the prospect of the sun's imminent return. Ellen and George Stanton were among those chatting with friends, both of them dressed in their Sunday best.

"Hello, dears." Ellen broke away from the group to greet her daughters. She hugged Abby, then bent to do the same to Mary. "We just heard this morning about your break-in. I wish you'd called us. We could have come over."

"There wasn't anything you could do, Mother." Mary held Ellen's hand. "Nothing was taken and no great harm done."

"Still, we could have been there for you."

George joined them. His wiry physique might not have been as strong as it once was, and his hair had long since gone from brown to whitish-gray, but he was still an imposing figure of a man. At the moment, his weathered features were drawn in concern.

"Are you girls all right?" he asked.

"We're fine, Dad."

He slipped his arm around Abby's waist. "Has Henry come up with any leads? We must have had three or four break-ins around town in the past few weeks."

"He's trying, but nothing yet. Mary did get a quick glimpse

of the thief. Once there are some suspects, she may be able to identify him."

"Well, you girls be careful."

"We will." Abby tipped her head to his shoulder in what she meant as a reassuring gesture, daughter to father. "Speaking of headline news, what's all this about you picketing the Senior Center?"

"Oh, it's nothing but some bureaucratic nonsense." He humphed his disapproval. "Dorthea Gilmore is an overly conscientious government dietitian who's got it in her head that we shouldn't have free donuts during the Men's Club meeting. She's threatening to withdraw funds for senior programs if we don't relent. It's ridiculous."

"Donuts probably aren't good for you, Dad. A lot of fat and sugar in them."

He shot her an annoyed look. "Abigail Stanton, I've been deciding what I will and will not eat for a good many years. My cholesterol is fine, my blood pressure is good and so is my weight, according to my doctor. A donut once a week is not going to hurt me or my friends. Furthermore, it's downright un-American for some government official to tell adults what they can and cannot eat."

Amused by her father's passionate outburst, Abby said, "I guess that means you're going to keep picketing."

"He's threatened to smuggle donuts into the Senior Center and hand them out clandestinely to his cronies," Ellen said.

"Well, it's our right," he grumbled.

Fortunately, the strains of the prelude drifted out to those who were still chatting with friends, calling the worshipers to service. The continuing saga of the proscribed donuts would have to wait for another time.

AFTER CHURCH, Mary and Abby followed their parents to the Stanton Farm for Sunday supper, their weekly custom. But Mary was visibly anxious about someone breaking into her house while they were gone, so they didn't linger long after eating and cleaning up the kitchen following supper.

Once back home, Abby went upstairs to her room. When she moved in with Mary, her sister had insisted she take the master bedroom since Mary could no longer climb the stairs. Abby had reluctantly agreed. To make it her own, she'd decorated the room in earth tones and hung her favorite watercolors of endangered birds on the walls. Her porcelain collection of birds, mostly gifts from friends, resided on her walnut-stained dresser where she could enjoy them every day—and dust them not quite as often as she should.

Now she pulled a chair up to her desk and powered up her laptop. She'd decided to check police reports on the Internet for break-ins with a similar MO, or modus operandi, on other islands in the San Juans. Perhaps she'd be able to find the illusive link she was looking for.

She first checked records for San Juan County, which included all of the islands. There'd been a break-in of an auto parts store in Friday Harbor a month ago. Not much was taken. The reporting deputy thought it likely someone was working on his own car and needed a new carburetor. There'd been one false alarm at a beauty shop. The owner had forgotten to set the alarm properly.

She'd started to check the records of towns on the mainland when Mary called her from downstairs. Bobby had come to see Abby.

Taking her glasses off, Abby rubbed her tired eyes, then went to see what her young neighbor was up to today. His clever mind was a bubbling cauldron of ideas and questions.

She found him sitting at the kitchen table, a shoe box in front of him. He'd changed out of his church clothes into jeans and a Seahawks T-shirt. His zippered sweatshirt hung open, and he was eating one of Mary's homemade chocolate chip cookies.

"If you're here to talk me into doing standup comedy with you and Mary, the answer is no," Abby teased.

"Now wait a minute," Mary interjected, setting a glass of milk in front of Bobby. "I'm not doing any standup either."

Bobby grinned, his eyes sparkling with mischief. "I think you both ought to, but that's not why I came to see you."

"Whew. That's a relief." Abby sat opposite the boy. "So what's up?"

"This." He pushed the box across the table. "I found these in the Wetherbees' vegetable garden down the street. They haven't planted anything this year yet, and I found these little cocoon things stuck on an old head of cabbage that they never harvested. I wanted to know what they'd turn into." He downed a big swallow of milk before selecting a second cookie.

Abby removed the lid on the shoe box. She loved how Bobby was curious about everything in nature. It was a marvelous trait in a young person.

"I'm not an expert in entomology but maybe I can make a guess." She peered inside and found several cabbage leaves. Gingerly, she picked one up. Two hard-shelled pupae were clinging to a leaf with several holes in it.

"I'd say this is either the pupa of a moth or a butterfly. It's like a cocoon. You can see where the caterpillar ate the leaf last summer before changing into the pupa state for the winter." She pointed out the damage to the leaves.

"Can you tell what kind of butterfly it is?"

"I'm afraid I'm not that good at identifying pupae. When they emerge, we should be able to find pictures of moths and butterflies, and determine what you have."

"How long before they emerge, do you think?"

Abby shrugged. "Depends on what species they are. Probably a few weeks. We usually get a big increase in butterflies in early spring."

His smooth forehead furrowed into a frown and he gnawed on his lower lip. "Mom says I shouldn't keep them in the box. They need light. And when they come out of their cocoons, they're going to want to fly. They can't do that in a shoe box."

"True. Does your mother have something like a glass terrarium or a large fish bowl?"

He shook his head. "I don't think so."

She glanced at Mary. "Do we have something like that?"

"We had goldfish when Zack and Nancy were young, but I gave the goldfish bowl away years ago." Mary's children had long since grown up and moved away, Nancy to Florida where she was raising her own children and Zack off pursuing his musical career with a jazz band.

"Well, let me think." She replaced the lid on the box. "There's an empty terrarium at the Nature Museum. If you'd like, I can take the pupae to work tomorrow. I'll put them in the terrarium and put a screen over the top so they get light and air, but can't fly away. We can put up a sign and let the museum visitors guess what the pupae will become."

He brightened immediately. "That'd be great. I can come by every day to check on 'em till they emerge."

"And then we'll release them so they can find somewhere to lay their eggs and start the cycle all over again," Abby said.

"Yeah, that'd be cool."

His youthful excitement was contagious, and Abby looked forward to his latest journey of discovery.

EARLY MONDAY MORNING, Abby arrived at the Nature Museum with Bobby's shoe box and a new resolve to uncover the identity of the Sparrow Island thief.

As she walked toward the building, she noticed the branches of the bigleaf maple that dominated the circular drive boasted telltale tips of green on its branches. Spring would soon arrive. As would Bobby's butterflies, she imagined.

Pulling open the heavy glass door, she stepped into the lobby. As usual, Wilma Washburn was already at work behind the receptionist's counter, her eyes glued on the computer screen.

"You're looking very intense this morning, Wilma."

The receptionist and the Nature Museum's general go-to gal looked up from the computer. "Good morning, Abby. Looks like you've brought a box lunch to work today." Wilma's welcoming smile brightened her whole face and made her look younger than her sixty-some years.

"Not lunch. A new Bobby McDonald project. He found some butterfly or moth pupae, and we're going to see what emerges."

"That youngster's something else, isn't he?"

"He is indeed." Abby gestured toward the computer screen, which was visible from where she stood. "Is that a new project you're working on?"

"It's a Family History Project sponsored by the Office of Indian Affairs. Researchers have spent months talking to tribal leaders to put together relationships and ancestry that goes back to the 1700s."

"That sounds interesting."

"It's been a massive project. What's really amazing are the links between various tribes here in the Northwest. Lots of intermarriages. With the early settlers too."

"Are you able to track your lineage in the study?"

"Oh, yes. But my family has passed down that information in our oral history for generations. The project managers have asked me to check to see that what they have is accurate. The lineage is more difficult to track in mixed tribal or racial families."

"Fascinating." Knowing your family history grounded a person and gave one a sense of belonging. "I'd love to hear more, but right now I'd better get to work."

Leaving Wilma to her history project, Abby pushed through a door marked PRIVATE that led to the offices and a workroom in the back where she worked with specimens and built displays. A red-tailed hawk's wing, which had been broken during cleaning, awaited repair on the long worktable.

Setting the shoe box aside, she found a step stool and climbed up to reach the five-gallon terrarium stored on top of a storage cabinet. It was a bit of a stretch.

"Why don't you let me get that for you?"

She started at the sound of Hugo Baron's voice and had to steady herself by grabbing the cabinet.

"Easy now," he warned.

"I'm fine." Smiling, she stepped down and faced her boss, the founder of the Sparrow Island Nature Conservatory. As was frequently the case, he was dressed nattily in a hand-tailored suit, white shirt and carefully knotted silk tie. "But I happily accept your offer. Your arms are significantly longer than mine."

Almost six feet tall, Hugo had a regal bearing that made her think of British nobility. His snow-white hair, matching mustache and carefully manicured fingernails, added to that image. But he was no pampered royal. He'd traveled the world, learning about many cultures and advancing conservation causes on every continent.

As agile as a much younger man, he climbed up and retrieved the terrarium.

"I assume you have some important use for this." He placed the container on the worktable.

"I do. A small entomology project inspired by Bobby McDonald." She showed him the pupae and explained what she planned to do.

"Excellent. Yet another way to get our visitors to think about nature."

"I thought so." She rummaged around beneath the worktable in search of a piece of screening with a fine enough mesh that it would keep the butterflies enclosed in the terrarium once they emerged.

She made sure the screen remnant she'd found was big enough to do the job, then carefully moved the cabbage leaves and pupae into the terrarium. Standing back, she checked the display and thought about what the sign should say.

"If I may suggest," Hugo said, "perhaps you could turn the learning experience into a contest. Those who guess correctly what will emerge could win some token prize. A certificate? Or one of our Nature Museum campaign buttons?"

"Good idea."

"Well, then, I'll let you get on with your work."

When he turned to leave, she stopped him. Discovering the identity of the Sparrow Island thief was very much on her mind, and Hugo might be able to help.

"As long as you're here," she said, "have you noticed any construction work going on around Green Harbor or anywhere on the island?"

"Construction?"

"Yes, we had a break-in at Mary's house."

His expression immediately turned to one of concern. "I'd heard there'd been some thefts, but I didn't know you and Mary had been affected. Was anything taken?"

She told him about the incident and the sketchy description of the culprit, a man wearing work boots. "I thought I'd nose around, see if I could turn up any leads."

"Ah, our own Miss Marple strikes again."

She laughed and felt heat color her cheeks. "I do seem to love a mystery, don't I?" Since she'd returned to Sparrow Island, she'd been fortunate to solve a few mysteries, which had more than a few people referring to her as the popular Agatha Christie character.

"I suspect Henry Cobb would do well to hire you as a deputy."

"I'll stick with my amateur status, thanks. But I'm stuck trying to think of any big construction projects going on recently."

"They've been doing some work at the marina lately. Extending one of the docks and repairing another one."

"Oh, right. I was thinking about house construction and had forgotten about the marina project." She boosted herself onto a stool by the worktable.

"Last week I had to take a detour because of some street work on the north side of the island. Would that qualify?"

"It might. Opal Collins mentioned a road resurfacing project in her neighborhood."

"Of course, most men own a pair of work boots. I certainly do, and I suppose your father does too."

"That's the problem, isn't it? I'm not likely to narrow the field of suspects much by questioning men wearing work boots." Or baseball caps, for that matter. Those were as ubiquitous as sea gulls on the island.

Still, she felt some urgency to keep trying. The thief could easily strike Mary's house again. As courageous as her sister might be, Mary was also confined to a wheelchair and therefore vulnerable.

That could make her an ideal target for a predatory criminal.

She decided after she had the terrarium display set up, she'd talk to Rick DeBow at the marina. Once a stockbroker, Rick had given up his high-pressure job and moved to Sparrow Island, where he'd become an all-purpose handyman around town. His talents included repairing boat engines, so he'd set up shop at the marina. With his sharp eye and innate intelligence, he'd have noticed any suspicious characters around the marina.

She found some poster board and hand-lettered a sign describing the contest. Then she made up some paper ballots, leaving space for the person to write his name, address, phone number and his guess. Although the Nature Museum didn't have huge numbers of visitors this time of year, they did get regular school tours. The kids would love a chance to win something.

Her task accomplished, she mentally put on her detective hat and headed out the door.

AS MANY AS A HUNDRED BOATS pulled gently on their mooring lines in the slips that lined both sides of the four wooden docks. Both cabin cruisers and sailboats rocked rhythmically in the swells. Sea gulls screeched from their perches on tall masts. Periodically, an alpha male would run a smaller bird off from the spot he wanted to claim.

During the summer months, the marina was a hive of activity, boats coming and going almost constantly. Now most of the boats were locked up tight and covered with royal blue canvas to protect them from the elements.

Walking toward the shed where Rick DeBow often did his work, Abby noted two heavy-duty pickup trucks parked near the dock. Both had the logo of H&C Construction on their doors. A third truck, a white one, was parked nearby.

She found Rick up to his elbows in grease with the parts of an outboard motor spread out over his workbench. Dressed in jeans and a faded flannel shirt with the sleeves rolled up, he wouldn't easily be taken for a former stockbroker.

"That looks like a jigsaw puzzle I'd never be able to put back together," she said.

He looked up from his work. "I'm never too sure about it myself."

"Oh dear." She chuckled.

Picking up a blue shop cloth, he wiped his hands. Although not tall, he was a muscular man, his brown hair curly and laced with gray.

"What brings you down to the marina on such a gray day? Planning a boat trip?" he asked.

"No, I'm investigating the recent break-ins around Sparrow Island." Once again she repeated what had happened at Mary's house. Because Rick was one of her many friends who had helped her solve other mysteries on the island, he showed no surprise that she was delving into the latest crime wave. "I'm convinced the thief isn't from Sparrow Island, because the robberies just started happening about two weeks ago. I'm investigating workmen who are strangers in town and have been working here over the past month or so. I thought you might have talked with the crew that's repairing the marina or might have heard or seen something suspicious."

He thought for a moment. "Like what, for instance?"

"I don't know. Maybe you've heard someone bragging about coming into some extra money. Or they've shown up with a new truck."

Slowly, he shook his head. "I haven't paid much attention to what's going on out there, except when they get their power saws going. Then I have to wear ear plugs. Other than that, the guys seem to come and go, minding their own business. I could introduce you to the contractor. He might have heard something."

"Sounds like a plan."

Together they walked down the dock to where two men were on their knees replacing a rotten crosspiece. A third, older man stood nearby talking on a cell phone. They stopped a few paces away until he finished his call.

"Hey, Rick, what's up?" the older man said.

"I'd like you to meet Abby Stanton. Hooper's the contractor on the dock repair job, Abby."

She shook Hooper's callused hand, roughened by years of hard work. "Mr. Hooper, I'm investigating some break-ins we've had here on the island. I'm hoping you might be able to identify a man we're looking for."

He slanted her a curious look. His eyes were a pale blue in a face weathered and wrinkled by years of exposure to the sun. "You're a cop?"

"No, but my house was broken into so I have a personal interest in making sure the thief is caught."

"I don't know anything about any break-in, lady."

"She isn't accusing you, Hooper," Rick said. "She just wants to ask you about your employees."

"I'm wondering if any of your men have been acting strange lately," she said. "Maybe bragging about having money or buying a new vehicle? Or acting secretive?"

One of the workmen dropped a crosspiece into place with a bang. His partner jumped back. "Hey, watch it, Barber!"

"My guys work hard, ma'am," Hooper said, "and I pay 'em the going wage. They wouldn't have a reason to break into somebody's place."

"I'm sure that's true. Then I assume you can account for where all your men were last Friday during the late afternoon."

"Look, lady, we all come over from Friday Harbor on the seven o'clock ferry and take the four thirty back home. They get a half hour for lunch. That's it."

"Then you could account for their time last Tuesday as well?" That was the day Margaret had been robbed.

"Every day it's the same schedule and will be 'til we're done with this job." Impatient, he turned and started to walk away, then stopped.

"You've thought of something?" Abby ventured.

He hesitated. "One of my guys . . . he's a good worker, but sometimes he doesn't go back to Friday Harbor with us. It probably doesn't mean anything. I mean, he's no kid. I don't keep 'em on a leash."

Abby felt a spurt of adrenaline. "Is he here? Could I talk with him?"

Not happy about her request, he glanced around. "Hey, Barber. Come here a sec."

Slowly, one of the two workmen stood. In his midtwenties, he wore a black T-shirt that revealed well-defined biceps covered with tattoos. A dark baseball cap sat squarely on his head, shaggy black hair sticking out beneath it. His work boots were scuffed and had thick soles.

"Yeah?" He turned his head away and coughed.

"This lady wants to talk to you." Hooper cocked his head in Abby's direction. "Darren Barber, Abby Stanton."

"Darren, could you tell me where you were last Friday afternoon." She noticed his tattoos weren't artistically drawn but somehow rough, as though the artist had been unskilled or in a hurry.

The young man glanced at his boss, then at Rick. "I was working. Mr. Hooper knows that."

"How about late afternoon, say four o'clock?"

He shrugged. "I dunno. Took the ferry back to Friday Harbor, I guess."

"Your boss said you didn't go back with him that day," Rick added.

"So?" Darren cleared his throat.

"How about Tuesday last week?" Abby asked. "Where were you that afternoon?"

"How should I know? I come to work and go home. What's the big deal?"

"There was an attempted robbery here last Friday and a

break-in that Tuesday. Maybe you know something about that?" Rick asked.

"I don't know nuthin' about no robbery." He appealed to Hooper. "Can I get back to work now?"

Hooper nodded his approval, but looked concerned. "He's been a good worker," he reiterated as the construction worker walked away.

Abby appreciated that. But Darren Barber fit Mary's description and he had no alibi for at least two of the incidents.

Henry Cobb would want to take a closer look at the young man.

CHAPTER ✿ FIVE

MARY SPENT MOST OF Monday working in her craft room. She'd intentionally stayed at home during the day, afraid the thief might return and if he did, determined to run him off and get a better look at him in the process. So far, it had been eerily quiet in the neighborhood.

Since the morning rush hour when her neighbors had gone off to work or school, few cars had passed by on the street. A UPS delivery truck had driven by before noon. She'd recognized Samson, the regular driver on the route. Happily married with two children, he lived on San Juan Island, and was an unlikely thief.

This afternoon, the mail carrier had waved at Mary through the window as she slid the mail into the box, then drove on to the neighbor's house. Another unlikely suspect.

All things considered, it had been an uneventful day. Blossom had spent most of it dozing on the windowsill in the craft room, Finnegan on the floor beside Mary's chair. Clearly she'd been worried over nothing. A few more days of staying at home and she'd go stir-crazy. She simply wasn't used to such a confined life.

Now the school bus roared by, stopping a half block down the street. The sound of children shouting drifted through the window along with the engine noise of the bus moving on to its next stop. The neighborhood seemed to come alive again.

Setting the sweater aside, Mary rolled back from the work-table just as the phone rang in the kitchen.

She froze for a moment.

This was about the same time of day when she'd awakened from a nap last Friday to find a man had broken into her house.

The phone rang a second time.

Quickly turning her chair, she wheeled toward the kitchen.

Perhaps it was the same person who had called last week. Twice, come to think of it. Both on Friday and then while Bobby had been here on Saturday.

She'd set the phone to ring five times before it switched to the answering machine. Many people hung up after the third or fourth ring. But Mary often couldn't get to the phone that soon.

Her friends knew that.

They also had her cell number.

A sense of foreboding urged Mary to hurry, to answer the phone before the caller hung up.

The phone rang for a third time.

Rolling into the kitchen, Finnegan right behind her, Mary wheeled past the table to the telephone stand and snatched up the instrument as the fourth ring began.

"Hello," she said, more breathless from anxiety than the exercise.

The hollow sound of emptiness greeted her. Then the phone clicked and she heard the dial tone. No one was there.

She stared at the phone in her hand. The tone continued to sound. The caller had hung up.

Cautiously, as though she were handling a dangerous snake, she cradled the phone. A sense of unease slid down her spine.

She wheeled to the back door. The glass glistened in the lowering rays of sunlight.

Who had called her? Why had they hung up as soon as she answered the phone?

A dog down the street started to fuss, his barks setting off a second dog.

The hair on the back of Mary's neck rose.

She reached for her cell phone.

MARY WATCHED out the front window for Henry's arrival. She felt foolish for calling him. But the call had frayed her already taut nerves, the hang up severing her common sense.

People dialed wrong numbers all the time. And they hung up when the wrong party answered.

She'd let her imagination take flight.

Henry's cruiser roared up to the front of the house and came to a jerking halt. He was out of the car by the time Abby's hybrid pulled into the driveway. She'd been at the sheriff's substation when Mary had reached Henry.

Mary wheeled into the front hall to open the door for them. Henry strode toward her with an air of determination.

"Anything?" His lips were drawn into a grim line. His hand rested on his holstered weapon.

Abby scurried across the lawn from where she'd parked her car.

"I'm afraid I cried wolf this time," Mary said. "I haven't seen a soul since I called you. I'm sorry I bothered you both."

"Don't be." Visibly relaxing, Henry glanced up and down the street. "You did the right thing by calling."

Abby took Mary's hand. "What specifically was it about the call that made you nervous? Did you hear something? Like background noise? Or heavy breathing?"

"Goodness no, not the heavy breathing part." Mary tried to recall if there'd been any sound at all before the party had disconnected. "I don't remember hearing a thing, but I felt *threatened* somehow. I know I'm being foolish. It was probably my imagination and a bad case of nerves."

"Have you got caller ID on the phone?" Henry asked.

Mary nodded. "Yes, we do."

"I'll check it." He stepped past her and headed into the kitchen.

As she followed Henry, Mary chided herself for not thinking of that right after the caller had hung up.

"Here's the number of your last caller." Standing over the phone, Henry read off the number and wrote it down in a notebook. "That sound familiar to either of you?"

"It's a local area code, but I don't recognize the number," Abby said.

Mary didn't either.

"Let's see if we can find out who it belongs to."

Using his own cell phone, Henry called the operator, asked for a supervisor and identified himself as doing police business.

"I'd like you to tell me who's listed for this number," he said when he'd been connected.

While Henry waited for an answer, Mary put on some

water to boil and got out some cups for tea. She'd caused Henry a needless trip, she was sure. He'd find out the caller was a legitimate business, or maybe even a friend she hadn't heard from in a long while who didn't have her cell number.

He thanked the operator and disconnected. "The call came from a throwaway cell phone. There's no way to tell who owns it."

"Can you trace where the call was made from?" Mary asked.

"No, that only happens if you can keep a caller on the phone for maybe five minutes. Then you can trace which cell towers the call goes through and get the general area it came from."

"I thought cell phones had GPS in them nowadays." Abby had taken a seat at the table, listening while Henry had made his call.

"Some do," he said. "But not the throwaway, prepaid models. They're bare bones, which is why criminals love to use 'em."

Goose flesh rose up along Mary's spine. "What about telemarketers? Do they use cell phones? I had another hang up on Saturday, and I didn't think much about it."

Henry's graying brows pulled together. "Telemarketers usually —but not always—work in a big room with dozens of lines coming in."

"So you think it was the robber calling me?" A lump of fear tightened Mary's throat.

"I have no idea, but I don't discount the possibility. Let's see if anyone answers." He punched in the number on his cell phone and waited. Within moments he disconnected. "The call went directly to voice mail, which hadn't been activated. Whoever owns the phone isn't interested in returning calls."

The water had begun to boil. Mary's hand trembled as she poured the water into a teapot to steep. Perhaps she hadn't imagined the unspoken threat after all.

Abby asked, "If you question a suspect and find he has a cell phone with that number in his possession, would that be evidence against him?"

"Only that he made the call here this afternoon. Not that he was the one who broke into the house."

"But you think there could be a connection?" Abby persisted.

He sat down at the table and waited until Mary delivered teacups to them.

"At this point, it's only conjecture," he said.

"Then what about questioning the man I told you about this afternoon?" Abby asked.

Using a tray she held in her lap, Mary brought the teapot to the table. "What man?"

"I was down at the marina and talked to the contractor who's in charge of dock repairs. He has a young man working for him who meets the description of the man you saw, and he didn't have an alibi. Darren Barber. Henry checked him out. Darren spent eighteen months in prison for breaking and entering."

"Then he's the one?" Mary asked.

Henry held up his hand. "Easy now, let's not jump to conclusions. Your description was pretty vague. It'd fit dozens of men here in the San Juans. Maybe hundreds."

"But you're going to question him," Abby said.

He picked up the pot and poured tea into Mary's cup first. "Not just yet. If he's our perp, I don't want to spook him before I get some solid evidence. He's been pretty smart so far, not leaving any clues."

"But you'll keep an eye on him," Abby prodded.

He filled Abby's cup and then his own, adding sugar to his and stirring slowly with the spoon.

"I'll keep a close eye on him, I promise."

THE FOLLOWING MORNING, Abby decided to see if she could locate the work crew that was resurfacing the streets on the island. Since Henry wasn't a hundred percent convinced Darren Barber was guilty of the break-ins, and neither was she, Abby wanted to continue her search for suspects.

She truly wished she had a better description to work with. But Mary's glimpse of the man had been fleeting.

An overcast sky blocked the sun, eliminating shadows and casting the town of Green Harbor in monochrome shades of gray. Even brightly colored geraniums in planter boxes along the street appeared pastel in the flat light.

As Abby drove past Holloway's Hardware, she noticed only one man sitting on the front porch. Usually there were a half-dozen older gentlemen who daily shared fish stories and other tall tales during their morning ritual. The solitary man wore heavy work boots and a dark jacket, but didn't fit Mary's description of the thief. Nor did she expect to find the thief biding his time on Holloway's porch. Finding a robber wouldn't be that easy.

She turned left on Primrose Lane, which took her to Municipal Street where the post office, bank and Senior Center were located. She slowed and pulled over to the curb when she spied a group of about thirty men marching on the sidewalk in front of the Senior Center. The hand-painted picket signs they carried read DONUTS ARE OUR RIGHT; OUTLAW THE DIET POLICE; and DONUTS—THE AMERICAN WAY.

"Oh my," she said out loud as she spotted her father in the group. Evidently the usual porch sitters at Holloway's had found a different way to spend their time.

Unable to repress a smile, she got out of the car and walked toward the protestors, who were chanting their slogans.

"WHAT DO WE WANT?" shouted her father through a megaphone.

"DONUTS!" his followers answered.

"WHEN DO WE WANT THEM?"

"NOW!"

A crowd had begun to form across the street. Some joined in the chanting or cheered the pickets on. Others simply appeared amused. Meanwhile, in the middle of the street William Jansen was busy snapping pictures for his newspaper.

"Hi, Dad," Abby said.

"Oh, hello." He flashed her a quick smile. "WHAT DO WE WANT?"

The pickets chorused their answer.

"Great turnout today," her father said. "WHEN DO WE WANT THEM?

"NOW!"

"Yes, I can see that." She also noted a middle-aged woman standing on the porch, her arms crossed, her expression dour. Presumably that was Dorthea Gilmore, the bureaucrat who had caused all the fuss by eliminating donuts at the Men's Club meetings.

"Mark my words, we'll wear Ms. Rules-and-Regulations down soon." He held the megaphone to his mouth again. "WHAT DO WE WANT?"

"At least you and your friends are getting some exercise."

She recognized several of the pickets, among them Gordon Siebert, who owned the jewelry store in town, Sam Arbogast, who worked as a handyman for her parents, and Steven Jarvis, the local bank manager. It seemed the movers and shakers were all involved, which meant the state bureaucrat would eventually have to concede the field of battle, if she knew anything about local politics.

"Well, have fun, Dad." She stood on tiptoe and kissed his cheek. "Always nice to see democracy at work."

He shot her another grin before shouting into the megaphone again.

Returning to her car, Abby made a U-turn to avoid the crowd of onlookers and William Jansen, who seemed oblivious to the cars that were trying to make their way along the street and were all but running him over.

She'd take a different route out to Opal Collins' neighborhood. She'd mentioned work crews had been in the area, and Abby hoped to locate them.

When she came upon a recently resurfaced section of road, she started glancing down side streets in the hope of catching a glimpse of the workmen. It didn't take long.

She parked next to a county truck at the end of the cul de sac that was blocked off and got a strong whiff of overheated tar when she got out of the car. Of the five men on the crew, three were watching the other two shoveling asphalt from the back of a truck into potholes. The two with shovels both looked young and healthy, and wore dark work shirts as well as baseball caps.

Picking out the oldest of the three men supervising the project, who she guessed was the foreman, she approached the group. The way the man's stomach hung out over the top of his belt suggested he hadn't done any actual physical labor in some time.

"Excuse me," she said. "Are you in charge here?"

He glanced at his co-workers, then said, "Yeah. What can I do for you?"

"I wanted to talk to you about some break-ins that have occurred in the neighborhood."

His eyes narrowed, and he indicated they should step away from his workmen. "What's this about break-ins?" he asked when he came to a halt.

Abby went through the history of the break-ins, the nearby incident at Opal's house and what had happened at Mary's house.

"I'm wondering if you've noticed any of your men spending more money than usual lately and if you can account for the whereabouts of your crew members late last Friday afternoon."

He scratched his head beneath his ball cap, his dark hair highlighted with streaks of gray. "I don't want to point a finger at any of my men."

"But based on my question, you think one of your men may be the man I'm looking for."

He shoved his hands in his pockets and shot a glance toward the two men with the shovels. "Look, I'm not saying Michael Romo is a thief. But you asked if I could account for his time last Friday, and the answer is no. He said he had to take off early to handle some business."

"What about the prior Tuesday? Did he work a full shift that day?"

Pulling his palm down his face, he rubbed his day-old

whiskers. "I'm not sure. I'd have to check his time card. But he's been taking a lot of time off lately. I had a talk with him about it. He claims whatever personal problem he's got is only temporary. I had to write him up and put the warning in his personnel jacket."

"Would it be all right if I talked with Michael?"

The foreman shrugged. "I guess." He walked a few paces toward the two men wielding shovels. "Hey, Michael. A lady wants to talk to you."

Both men looked toward their boss. The shorter of the two, who had dark hair and an olive complexion, straightened and glanced toward Abby. Something flickered in his eyes.

Suddenly, he dropped his shovel right where he stood and bolted toward one of the houses on the cul de sac. He raced down the driveway, then ducked through a hedge of rhododendrons and ran out of sight into a wooded area.

"I'd say that kid is guilty of something," the foreman concluded.

Abby agreed. "Does he live here on the Island?"

"Nah, he lives in Bellingham. Takes the ferry over every morning."

Curious about what had made Michael run, the other workmen edged closer to their boss.

Abby plucked her cell phone from its holster on her belt. Henry would want to talk to that young man. "Do you know Michael's address?"

"I don't have it. But the county Human Resources office at Friday Harbor would."

As she walked back to her car, Abby punched in Henry's number. He answered on the first ring, and she told him about Michael.

"Abby, you can't go around accosting men just because they're wearing work boots and dark shirts. You've got to have some reason to question a person."

"You have a reason now, Henry."

His grunt in response suggested he wasn't pleased with the idea.

AFTER TALKING WITH HENRY, Abby drove to the Nature Museum. She had some paperwork to do, including preparations for the annual spring survey of trees on the conservatory grounds to check for broken limbs or disease. Henry would have to decide for himself how vigorously to pursue either Michael Romo or Darren Barber. For herself, she'd like to know if either of them owned the cell phone that had made the call to Mary's house.

She walked into her office and hung her jacket on the back of the door. Sitting down at her walnut desk, she dropped her purse into the bottom drawer, then turned to the mail that was in her in-box. A flyer announced the opening of a new display at Cornell's Lab of Ornithology. She smiled, proud of the institution's continued accomplishments. While she still missed some of her friends there, she was glad God had led her back home to Sparrow Island after so many years away.

Bobby McDonald burst in through the doorway.

"Hi, Abby. The terrarium with the pupae looks neat. I didn't know you were going to turn it into a contest." He plopped himself down on the visitor's chair next to her desk. His zippered sweatshirt hung open and there was a stain on the T-shirt underneath, probably from a spill at lunch. His mother wouldn't send him to school in a dirty shirt. What happened later . . . well, that wasn't a mother's fault.

"The contest was Hugo's idea. He thought that would encourage visitors to ask more questions."

"Super. Is it okay if I enter the contest too?"

"I don't see why not. After all, it's really your display. The prize isn't going to be anything big, though."

"That's okay. I just like to win contests."

Abby did find Bobby to be quite competitive, but always in a healthy way. If he won something, it was because he worked hard for the prize.

The door swung open again, and Hugo strolled in.

"I thought I heard Master McDonald's voice. How are you, young man?" He extended his hand and Bobby took it.

"I'm great, thank you, and I'm going to enter the pupae contest."

"Good for you."

"I'm going by the library on the way home and see if they've got a book on butterflies and moths. Maybe it'll show a pupa stage and I can win the contest."

"Very clever of you to look up the answer in a book," Hugo said, giving Abby a wink.

Bobby hopped up from the chair. "I'm good at contests. In fact, I'm going to enter the Springhouse Café contest for the best standup comic so I can win some brunch tickets for my parents. I'm making up my own jokes . . . well, with Mary's help. You ought to enter, too, Mr. Baron."

"Me?" Hugo's blue eyes widened and his mustache quivered as he tried to suppress a smile. "I don't believe I'd be very good at standup comedy."

"Be careful, Hugo," Abby warned. "Bobby can be persuasive. I think he's almost convinced Mary to enter the contest with her own original jokes."

"You'd be great, Mr. Baron. I've heard you tell knock-knock jokes, and I always laugh at those."

"I appreciate your confidence in my abilities, young man. But I'm afraid knock-knock jokes are about the limit of my repertoire when it comes to humor."

"It's easy to make up stuff that's funny. I could help you."

Hugo rested his hand on the boy's shoulder. "Perhaps another time."

"I'll come by tomorrow after school to check on the pupae and make a guess, if I can find out what they are in a library book. If you're here, we can write some jokes together."

"Yes, well, we'll see."

"Great. I'll see you both tomorrow. Gotta get to the library before it closes." As though jet propelled, he rocketed out the door.

Hugo watched the boy leave, then turned back to Abby. "I have seen category four hurricanes with less stored up energy than that boy. He's a true force of nature."

Repressing a smile, Abby leaned back in her chair. "Did I just hear you agree to perform standup comedy at the Springhouse Café?" That would be a sight worth seeing.

Hugo sputtered a denial. "Nothing of the sort. In fact, rest assured I plan to be somewhere else tomorrow afternoon."

Abby suspected Hugo didn't fully appreciate how determined Bobby McDonald could be. He'd stalk Hugo until the man relented. Which was fine with Abby.

Bobby would stop wasting his boundless energy on trying to convince her to perform a standup routine as well.

CHAPTER ✿ SIX

Abby spent the next hour finishing up her paperwork, but her thoughts were never far from the rash of break-ins on the island, the strange hang-up phone calls Mary had received and the cell phone that couldn't be traced back to the owner. Even as she called it quits for the day and walked out to her car, something told her she was missing a clue. One part of the puzzle was right in front of her, yet she couldn't see it.

She pressed the remote to unlock the car doors, then stood staring into the twilight. An eagle swooped out of the sky, landing lightly in the nest near the top of a broken fir tree. Abby caught the gleam of a fish in his talons. *Dinnertime for his partner*, she thought with a smile. Soon there'd be hatchlings chirping for their fair share of the day's catch.

Then it hit her with the force of a revelation. The thief always broke into empty houses. Because he *called* first to make sure no one was home. Mary was the one exception. She couldn't get to the phone in time to pick up while he was on the line last Friday. So he'd mistakenly thought it was safe to break in. He thought he wouldn't be caught.

But he had been.

Abby's palms began to sweat as she tried to open the car door and found it had automatically relocked itself. She pressed the remote again.

If her theory was right, the thief was still targeting Mary's house. That's why there'd been two more hang-up phone calls.

She slid into the driver's seat. Henry didn't like her jumping to conclusions. That was understandable. So how could she prove her theory was right?

Margaret Blackstock had mentioned getting crank calls from teenagers. Maybe they weren't crank calls at all, but the thief checking to see if the coast was clear.

As for the other victims, Brenda Wilson and her husband had been out of town when the break-in occurred. If the thief had called their house, they wouldn't know about it.

No one had been home at the Brisbin house during the robbery. Both Belinda and her husband worked long hours. But maybe their daughter Summer had experienced a hang-up call in the days before the break-in. She often worked nights as a waitress at Winifred's, the nicest restaurant in town.

Abby glanced at her watch. It was getting late, but maybe she could catch Belinda at Beach Bag Books before she closed up.

On Shoreline Drive, the quaint lantern street lights were on, but the street was nearly deserted as Abby pulled up in front of the bookstore. She spotted Belinda moving around inside putting dust covers over the merchandise. The sign on the door said Closed.

Hopping out of her car, Abby hustled up to the door and rapped on the glass.

"Belinda, it's me. Abby Stanton."

Turning, Belinda squinted toward the door, then smiled in recognition. She unlocked the door.

"Goodness, have you suddenly run out of books to read?" She opened the door so Abby could step inside.

Abby laughed. "No, my to-be-read-pile is still gigantic. But I do have another question about your break-in."

"Oh?" She closed the door and locked it again. "I really haven't thought of anything I didn't tell you or Sergeant Cobb." Picking up a long cloth, she unfolded it over the display of best sellers in the front window.

"I'm wondering if you or your husband or maybe Summer received any phone calls in the days before your break-in when the caller hung up as soon as you answered."

Thoughtfully, Belinda pushed her glasses back up on her nose. "A hang-up call? I don't remember anything like that. Why do you ask?"

Abby described her theory to Belinda. "I think the thief may be checking to see if anyone's at home before he breaks in."

"I see." She nodded in understanding. "Gary didn't mention getting any calls like that, but he probably wouldn't."

"How about Summer?"

"Our work hours are opposite. And when she's not working, she's often out with her friends. We go days without seeing each other. I'm lucky to hear her come in at night after her shift at Winifred's."

"Could you ask her? And Gary?"

"I will. And I'll let you know what they say."

"If there's a connection with the phone calls, then maybe we can figure out where the thief will strike next. At least we can warn people to be wary if someone hangs up when they answer the phone."

Belinda picked up her purse from behind the counter and switched off the overhead lights. "Summer would sure like it if you caught the guy and she could get her computer back. She lost her whole address book, which means she doesn't have the e-mail addresses of her school friends."

"I'm hoping we catch him soon too." In large part because she suspected the thief hadn't given up on the idea of breaking into Mary's house.

She wondered what he could be after that was so valuable that he'd keep trying.

"I'VE BEEN TRYING TO WRITE some comparison jokes." Sitting at the kitchen table opposite Mary, Bobby flipped open his yellow notepad.

"You mean like comparing short and tall people?" Mary wasn't sure that would be all that funny.

"No, not really. See, you take two things you know about. Like I took butterflies and kids. Then you compare how they're alike and turn it into a joke."

Mary shook her head. "I'm not getting it." More evidence that she hadn't been born to do standup comedy.

"Here, I'll show you." He glanced at his notes. "My mom says raising a kid is like watching the life cycle of a butterfly. First the egg gets laid, then it turns into a voracious—that's a new word Mom taught me." His grin widened and his hazel eyes twinkled. "Anyway, it turns into a voracious caterpillar that eats everything in sight for the next twenty years. Finally, about the time you run out of stuff to eat, it turns into a butterfly that goes off to start its own family."

Mary smiled fondly at the boy. "That's very nice, Bobby. Did your mother really say that?"

"Well, no. I made it up while I was reading a book about butterflies. Guess it's not too funny, huh?"

"Not one of your best jokes, I'm afraid. But a sweet sentiment."

"Mom actually says I eat like I've got a hollow leg."

"My son Zack had a leg just like that." She smiled at the memory of Zack as a teenager. "I thought I'd never get him filled up. What I needed was a conveyor belt directly from the Green Grocer to his place at the dinner table. I couldn't keep enough food in the house for him."

Bobby giggled. "I'll ask Dad if he can make me one of those and have Mr. Goodfellow put gallons of ice cream on the conveyor belt."

Mary looked up when she heard the garage door open, then glanced at the clock. Abby was home.

Earlier, Mary had put a roast in the oven and a small zucchini and cheese casserole. Abby's timing was excellent.

She scooted back from the table. "Young man, you'll have to excuse me. I have a salad to make . . . unless you'd like to help me chop some celery and carrots?"

Bobby closed up the notepad where he'd been writing his jokes. "I would, Mary, but I'd better get home. Mom will wonder where I am."

"And suspect I've been filling your hollow leg, I imagine," she teased.

He looked marginally embarrassed. "Only a couple of cookies and some milk."

"Tell your mom hello for me."

He scooped up his notepad and pencil, and slipped out the back door just as Abby came into the kitchen through the garage. She saw the door close behind the boy.

"I hope I didn't interrupt something important," she said.

"Only the great joke-writing fest, which continues unabated, I'm afraid. Although not always productive." Mary thought briefly how at night, when she was trying to go to sleep, silly jokes popped into her head, which she sometimes forgot by morning. Perhaps tonight she'd come up with one of those comparison jokes Bobby was working on.

Abby slipped off her jacket. "Did you have any more of those hang-up phone calls today?"

"As a matter of fact, I did get a call a little after noon. But it was a different phone number this time." Mary caught the concern in Abby's face. "Is that good or bad?"

"I'm not sure." Removing her glasses, she cleaned them with the corner of a fresh tea towel. "Did you write down the number?"

"I did. Then I called Henry. He's going to check it out, see who's listed with that number. The area code was Toledo, Ohio."

"Toledo? Good grief! Who'd be calling you from Toledo?"

"I have no idea. But I didn't want to call back without knowing whose phone it was."

"Good idea."

Then, to Mary's distress, Abby explained that she thought the hang-up calls meant her house was still on the thief's target list. He wanted something. Here. Specifically. In her house.

But what? And who on earth from Toledo would want to rob her house?

BEFORE BREAKFAST Wednesday morning, Abby made it a point to go outside to get the newspaper. She imagined William had written an article about Mary's break-in. She wanted to know, too, if there had been any other incidents.

To her surprise, the *Birdcall* hadn't arrived. Squatting down, she looked under the rhododendron bush by Mary's bedroom window in case Lynell Cowan had thrown it there in error. She frowned. It wasn't there either. *Odd.* Lynell was very faithful about delivering the paper. Now he'd missed their house two weeks in a row.

She glanced up the street and saw Sandy McDonald in her front yard.

Abby called to her. "Did you get your paper this morning?"

"No, that's what I was looking for." She walked toward Abby. "You didn't get one either?"

"Nope. I wonder if Lynell's been ill. He's never forgotten us before, except for last week."

Sandy looked up and down the street. "I wonder if he skipped anyone else on the street. Or maybe someone's stealing our papers."

"With all due regard to William and the *Birdcall,* why would anyone want to steal our newspapers?"

"To wrap a lot of fish in?" she said with a teasing grin. "Well, I've got to get to work, paper or not. Have a good day."

"Thanks. You too. I'll call William and let him know we've been skipped again." The Case of the Missing Newspapers wasn't a mystery she felt a need to solve. She'd leave that to William.

She was far more concerned about the break-ins and intended to talk to Opal Collins again this morning.

She went back into the house, picked up the phone in the kitchen and dialed the number for the *Birdcall*. To her surprise, William answered on the first ring.

After she identified herself, she said, "I didn't expect to find you at the office so early, William. I was going to leave a message."

"I'm still at home. I get call forwarding. You never know when there's going to be breaking news around here."

"Of course." She smiled to herself. The level of excitement on Sparrow Island typically included births, deaths and the library's used-book sale. The recent robberies were an exception. "I wanted to let you know we didn't get our paper again this morning and neither did the McDonalds."

"That's crazy. I talked to Lynell last week. He swore he delivered to both you and the McDonalds."

"I don't know what to say, William. The paper's not here. I even looked under the bushes."

She heard him muttering to himself. "I'll get to the bottom of this, Abby, and personally deliver your paper to your house later this morning. I can't have our subscribers not getting their papers."

AFTER A BREAKFAST of banana-nut muffins, orange juice and coffee with Mary, Abby headed out for Opal's house. The weather had improved considerably. Although the temperature was only in the fifties, the sky had cleared, leaving a few scattered clouds as a reminder of the overcast that had lingered for days.

Thank You, Lord, for the gift of sunshine. Abby's spirits always improved on sunny days and her heart filled with gratitude for all that the Lord had given her.

She'd barely made it to the end of the block when her cell phone rang. She pulled over to answer the phone and heard Margaret Blackstock's excited voice.

"I've caught those little mischief makers," she said. "I've got them right here in my office. They've confessed to everything."

Confused, Abby frowned. "What mischief makers?"

"Why, the ones who've been making all those crank calls and then breaking into people's houses and taking things they shouldn't. Shame on them, I say."

Still not following well, Abby said, "You mean they're students in Green Harbor Public School?"

"Sixth graders. You know how smart-alecky twelve-year-old boys can be. I'm going to call Sergeant Cobb. He'll take care of—"

"No, wait." This made no sense. Mary had seen an adult male fleeing her house, not a young adolescent. "I'll be right there. Hold onto the boys until I can talk to them."

"They've already admitted—"

"I'll be there in less than ten minutes. I'm in my car now." Abby flipped her phone closed and pulled away from the curb.

She supposed twelve-year-olds could break into homes and steal whatever they could find. But the current rash of robberies seemed too organized. Too targeted to homes that had cash on hand or valuable property.

How would a bunch of kids dispose of something like a silver tea service? There wasn't a pawn shop in Green Harbor. And surely if they somehow took the stolen goods to a pawn shop on the mainland, the owner would become suspicious.

After pulling up to the school, Abby hurried up to the main

door and rushed down the corridor to the principal's office. Three boys sat slumped on chairs against one wall. They all wore hooded sweatshirts and jeans, which might match Mary's description of the thief if they hadn't all looked so terribly young.

Margaret was behind her desk keeping an eye on the boys. She popped to her feet when Abby arrived.

"I caught 'em red handed. They called my house last night, making pests of themselves. Said something ridiculous about my refrigerator running and then hung up. But I had 'em dead to rights this time."

"How?" It sounded like a silly crank call to Abby.

"I've got caller ID. I checked the number and came in early this morning. I looked up their home numbers in my files, and Mr. Ryan Pilcher's home phone just happens to be the same number that called me. Isn't that right, Ryan?"

The boy in the middle shrugged and continued to study the tips of his scuffed running shoes. The laces were untied.

"Is it all right if I talk with them?" Abby asked.

"Knock yourself out."

Abby pulled a chair over in front of the boys and sat down. She studied the youngsters a moment before speaking.

"Who wants to tell me what this is all about?"

Three pairs of eyes flicked toward Abby and then slid away again.

The boy on the right spoke up. "All we do is make phone calls when we get bored. It's no big deal."

"Who do you call?" she asked.

"Anybody. You know, like the football coach. Or Mrs. Blackstock," Ryan said.

"Sometimes we call Mr. Willoughby at the drugstore. He always falls for that old one about being from the power company and would he check to see if the street light's out in front of his store."

The kid on the left snorted a laugh. "He always goes out and checks. Weird dude."

"You've never stolen anything from him or anyone else?" she asked.

The boys looked surprised, and shook their heads.

Abby thought about the calls to Mary's house. "Do you boys have your own cell phones?"

All three nodded.

She pulled out a small notepad from her jacket pocket, which she always carried in order to record any unexpected bird sightings.

"Tell me what your phone numbers are." She wrote down their answers. None of their numbers had appeared on Mary's caller ID. Certainly, none of them had Toledo area codes.

Leaning back in the chair, she perused Margaret's would-be crooks. Just kids with too much time on their hands, she concluded.

"Tell you what, I think if you apologize to Mrs. Blackstock for bothering her at home and promise you won't ever make those kinds of calls again, that she won't have the sheriff come question you. You'll be able to make it up to her by doing something around the school."

"Like what?" Ryan asked, slanting a look in Margaret's direction.

Margaret thought for a moment. "I've noticed there're a lot of loose papers blowing around the play yard and the sand in the sandbox is being traipsed out of where it belongs. You stay after school today and clean it up. We'll call it even."

"After school?" the boys complained.

"Having a chat with Sergeant Cobb is your other choice," Abby pointed out.

After some muttered conversation among the boys, they agreed to the conditions of their release. They apologized to Margaret and promised to stay after school.

When the boys left for their classroom, Margaret exhaled a discouraged sigh. "I was so sure the boys were guilty of the robberies, I would have bet on it."

"Then it's just as well you're not into gambling."

"True," she agreed.

The problem of who the culprit was remained, however. Abby was still hoping that Opal Collins could help her with that.

CHAPTER ✿ SEVEN

THE FIR TREES AND PINES glistened in the morning sunlight along Cross Island Road. Dandelions had begun blooming along the verge of the road, creating a butter-yellow path. Definite signs of spring were in the air.

Abby pulled into the driveway at Opal's house and walked up to the porch. The same black cat was curled up in the wicker chair. This time the cat hopped down and wound his way around Abby's legs, purring.

"Well, good morning to you too," Abby said as she rang the bell. She bent down to pet the cat's soft fur.

Opal opened the door. "Well, it appears Barabbas is in a friendly mood this morning."

Still petting the cat, Abby looked up at Opal, who had on a navy blue dress and yet another handmade sweater, this one knitted in bright, variegated colors. "Barabbas?"

"I rescued him from the pound in Bellingham. Saved him from certain death, and he's been a faithful companion since.

My only regret is that he likes to prowl around my bed at three o'clock in the morning and wake me up. So I lock him in the kitchen at night."

"I can understand why three o'clock visits would be a problem," Abby said, getting to her feet. "I stopped by to ask you another question about your robbery. I hope I haven't come at a bad time."

"I'm due to volunteer at the library this afternoon when all the children come in to do their homework, but now is fine." She stepped aside so Abby could enter.

The house smelled of cinnamon, and Abby noticed a bright red candle burning on the counter this time.

"Do you recall getting any hang-up phone calls before the robbery?"

"Oh, dear, let me think." She fiddled with the knickknacks on an end table, rearranging the tiny wood and ceramic figurines. "A day or two before the break-in—I think it was that Tuesday—I was outside when I heard the phone ring. I like to garden a bit, though I can't do as much as I used to. Anyway, I hurried inside, but the answering machine had already picked up. I grabbed the phone and said hello." Her forehead furrowed as she recalled the incident. "No one answered me, but I thought I heard someone on the other end of the line. Then I got the dial tone."

Abby felt a spurt of excitement. "Do you mean your answering machine recorded the call?"

"I suppose so, until the person hung up. I really don't know."

"Did you erase the message?"

"Why I . . . Let's take a look. I sometimes forget to erase my messages. People know to call me back if I don't call them."

Abby followed her into the kitchen where her answering machine was located on the corner of the white tile counter with a blue backsplash. At the end of the maple cupboards were half-circle maple shelves filled with collectable teacups and saucers on display.

Opal peered at the answering machine as though she thought it was a creature from outer space. "It looks like there're three messages here I haven't erased."

"Can you play them?"

"I think so." She pushed a button and a woman's voice reminded Opal about a meeting of the cultural arts group she was to attend last week.

That message was followed by one that had Opal's voice saying hello, then some background noise and a masculine cough so heavy with phlegm it made Abby's skin crawl. After that a dial tone sounded.

"That's the one!" Opal said.

"Wait." Abby held up her hand.

They listened to the next message, which was from Al Minsky, the owner of the local garage, telling Opal her car was ready.

"I had Al do a tune-up the other day," she explained. "He called me when my car was ready to pick up. A neighbor drove me over to get it."

"Let's listen to that second message again."

The tape rolled through the cultural arts message. Abby strained to hear the background noise on the second message. There was a grinding sound. Then the faint sound of high-pitched voices, and a cough that sounded as though the caller was getting over a very bad chest cold. Or he was a heavy smoker.

"Can you make out what that noise is?" Abby asked. "Right before the cough?"

Opal shook her head. "I have no idea."

"Is there a way to turn up the volume on your answering machine?"

"If there is, I don't know how. I'm rather technically challenged."

To some extent, Abby was limited in her technical abilities as well. At least as far as electronics went.

"What about caller ID? Do you have that service?"

"Oh, no, I don't see any reason to pay extra for that. If I'm here, I answer the phone. Sometimes I get into long conversations with telemarketers. That's not an easy job, you know, and if I'm lonely, I like to visit with them."

Abby imagined being a telemarketer wasn't easy, considering the money was poor and callers probably got yelled at a lot. But that didn't mean she enjoyed having her dinner interrupted by someone trying to sell her a set of golf balls. She'd always wondered how she got on that particular marketing list since she'd never played the game.

"Would you mind if I took the tape from your machine to Henry Cobb? Maybe he can enhance the sound and tell us what's there. It might give us a clue as to who our thief is."

"You're welcome to it if you can figure out how to get the tape out of the machine. I certainly don't know how."

Abby fussed with the machine and finally found the latch that popped it open. Gingerly she removed the small tape.

"I'll get this back to you as soon as I can," she said.

"No rush. Since half the time I forget to see if I have any messages, I won't miss it a bit. I'd far rather you catch whoever stole my mother's silver pieces."

"I'll do my best," Abby promised.

Since the Nature Museum was close by, Abby decided to stop there before taking the answering machine tape to Henry. She had a pretty convincing argument now that the thief was making sure the coast was clear before he broke into a house. Maybe now Henry would talk to the two suspects she'd turned up and see if they owned the cell phone that had called Mary's house.

A big yellow school bus parked in front of the Nature Museum indicated a group of youngsters on a field trip had arrived for a tour. One of the conservatory's talented volunteer docents would be explaining the exhibits to them this morning.

Abby pulled open the heavy glass door and went inside. Wilma was behind the reception desk, staring off into some middle distance. She didn't smile or greet Abby in any way. Getting an uneasy feeling in the pit of her stomach, Abby approached the counter.

"You look as though you've lost your best friend," Abby said.

Wilma started and blinked. Her eyes were red rimmed.

"Are you all right?" Abby asked, concerned.

"Not really." She was wearing her long, gray hair in a single braid and it draped over the front of her shoulder. She tugged on the tip absent-mindedly. "My house was broken into yesterday. They took a ceremonial wolf mask that was handed down from my great-great-grandfather. He was a famous woodcarver among the Salish people." Wilma's eyes filled with tears. "Why would they take something like that? Why couldn't they just take cash? Or my TV set? Something that wouldn't matter so much?"

"I'm so sorry, Wilma." Abby's heart went out to her friend,

and she took Wilma's hand in hers. "There's been a rash of break-ins lately. It's terrible."

Wilma nodded and tried to blink the tears away. "I read about them in the *Birdcall*, then Henry told me last night when he came to investigate—" Her voice broke. "I'm such a sentimental fool about that old cedar mask."

"Was it very valuable?"

"I don't know. Years ago, Tucker Billings suggested I get an appraisal and add it to my homeowner's insurance as a rider."

An independent insurance agent in Green Harbor, Tucker Billings had taken over the business from his father when he retired. "What value did you put on it?"

"I'm not even sure. Maybe a thousand dollars. But in terms of what that mask meant to me, my family and my tribal heritage?" She shook her head. "Priceless."

Again, Abby told Wilma how sorry she was. "Do you have any idea what time the break-in occurred?"

"Some time after twelve thirty. I'd dashed home on my lunch break to get the phone number of a friend in Seattle that another friend was trying to track down. I didn't have it here with me at the office. Everything was fine at home then. But by the time I got home after five, my back door was broken in and I was missing the mask and about two hundred dollars in cash."

The MO sounded exactly the same as the other Green Harbor break-ins.

"Did you get any calls while you were there?"

Wilma looked puzzled by the question. "No. I was just in and out again. I wasn't home for more than five minutes before I came back to the museum. One of our volunteers was staffing the desk for me."

"How about in the past week or two? Has anyone called and then hung up when you answered?"

"I don't think so. I'm really not home that much, except at night. Why are you asking?"

Abby told Wilma about her theory that the phone calls were the thief's way to check if the coast was clear. Although this was risky, so far the thief had gotten lucky.

"Very clever of him," Wilma said grimly.

"At least it's better than the thief having a confrontation with a victim and someone getting hurt." Mentally processing what she knew about the break-ins and the robber, she glanced at the large calendar on the wall behind Wilma. A training session for docents was scheduled in a couple of weeks. "How about your answering machine? Any strange calls there?"

"No. Most of my friends know to call me here at work during the day. Or, more likely, call me at home in the evening."

The group of what appeared to be third graders appeared from the exhibit area, led by a conservatory volunteer and their classroom teacher.

"It's a squished worm!" one child insisted to another.

"No, it's going to be a butterfly."

"It looks like bird poop to me."

Abby swallowed a grin, realizing the youngsters had seen the display of pupae and were making guesses about what, if anything, it would become.

"All right, children," the volunteer said, quieting them. "We're going outside now. And what are we going to look for?"

"Birds!" the youngsters chorused.

"What kind of birds?"

"Eagles," came the response.

"What other birds?"

"Sparrows."

"Excellent. There are lots of sparrows here on Sparrow Island." The volunteer smiled at her young charges. "And what do we have to do to hear the sparrows talking to each other?"

Her question was met with puzzled silence.

"You're absolutely right again." She leaned forward conspiratorially and held her finger to her lips. "We have to be very, very quiet so we don't frighten the sparrows away and we can listen to how they talk to each other."

Abby smiled to herself. The volunteer was doing a good job with the children. They'd remember their field trip for a long time and have a better appreciation of nature because of the docent's efforts.

As the children filed out of the building, she turned back to Wilma. "I'm going to go see Henry now. We've got to find out who's committing these robberies and stop him."

"Amen to that."

"If Hugo's looking for me, tell him what I'm up to."

"I will. But he won't be back in the office today. He had an appointment in Seattle and was going to stay through lunch."

"Are you still working on the Family History Project?"

"Huh?" Wilma blinked as though she'd forgotten about that. "Oh, yes. My part's pretty well completed. The amazing thing was how many distant cousins I have that I didn't even know about. You'd be surprised who's related to who around here. Turns out my family tree has a lot of branches."

"All of them resilient, I'm sure." Abby gave her friend an encouraging smile, then walked out to her car.

DRIVING INTO TOWN, Abby sent up a quick prayer. *Please, Lord, help us to stop this criminal before someone gets hurt.* While she appreciated that the losses the victims had experienced were personally painful, the situation would be even more dire if any of them had been injured during the course of the robberies. Criminals often escalated their level of violence, either accidentally or through their growing confidence and sense of invincibility.

That could lead to a very bad situation.

To Abby's surprise, she had to park nearly a block away from the sheriff's substation. She assumed there must be something going on at the school across the street, although the school parking lot didn't look full. That seemed odd.

When she opened the door to the sheriff's office, however, she discovered the action was there. Fully a dozen people were crowded into the room, all of them agitated and talking at once. Behind the counter, Henry Cobb was trying to listen to their complaints, and it looked like Mike Bennett was the deputy on duty this morning.

William Jansen stood off to the side taking notes, no doubt for an article in the newspaper's next edition.

"We've got to have more deputies here on Sparrow Island."

"Nobody's safe any more. Not even in their own home."

"What are you doing to protect us, Henry?"

"I never see a patrol car on my street. All your deputies do is drink coffee at the Springhouse Café."

Scowling at that remark, Henry held up his hand to silence the angry crowd. "Hold on, folks. I know you're all worried about these break-ins. So am I, and we're doing all we can to identify the person, or persons, committing the robberies."

"It's been going on for more than two weeks, Henry." Archie Goodfellow, wearing his Green Grocer apron, was right up front. "You don't even have a suspect yet."

"Can't you get some help from the county? An expert or something?" an elderly woman asked.

"Ma'am, my men are well trained, and we're working the case as hard as we can."

"There ought to be more deputies here," Frank Holloway said. Much shorter than Archie, but with a muscular build, the owner of the hardware store had shoved his way up to the counter as well.

Looking exasperated, Henry said, "Frank, you know as well as I do that the county commissioners set the budget for this office. I've got money for five deputies. You want any more assigned here, talk to the commissioners and the county sheriff. You elect them."

"We can unelect 'em too," the older woman muttered.

"All right, we'll talk to the commissioners," Archie said. "They'll hear us loud and clear."

"We'll have to get the whole town council to back us," Frank said.

"You're right," Archie agreed. "I'll call a town council meeting for tomorrow night. We'll meet in the Community Center." As the chairman of the council, he had the authority to call meetings.

"Wait!" William Jansen waved his hand to get their attention. "You can't call a public meeting without a public notice in the *Birdcall.* It's against the law."

"This is an emergency," Frank said.

"We aren't going to wait for your fool paper to come out next week," Archie groused. "Another dozen houses could be robbed by then."

"That's right," the others loudly agreed.

Abby thought a dozen possible break-ins in the next week was an exaggeration. But already there'd been six break-ins, including the failed attempted robbery at Mary's house.

"We can put up some posters around town," Frank insisted. "That's a good enough announcement. The word will get out about the meeting. People will come. You can bet on it. It sure won't be a secret meeting."

Abby imagined that if the rest of the town was as upset and fearful as those who were here hassling Henry, they'd have a packed room for the town council meeting.

"And we want you to give us a full report of what you're doing to stop these break-ins, Henry," Archie added.

"I'll be there." Henry didn't look happy about being ordered to appear before the Town Council.

The decision to call a town council meeting seemed to mollify everyone except William, who continued to object to the lack of public notification. He lost the argument, however, when Archie and Frank left. The restive crowd followed them out the door, leaving only Abby and William remaining on the civilian side of the counter.

William slid his notepad and pen back into his pocket. "I talked to Lynell. He swears he delivered papers to you and the McDonalds' both this morning and last week."

"If that's true, then they vanished into thin air by the time Sandy and I went out to get them."

His bushy brown eyebrows lowered into a scowl. "I think Lynell may be getting senile. I called a couple of other subscribers on your block. They haven't been getting their papers either, though they hadn't bothered to tell me about it." With his thumb and finger, he made an effort to smooth his mustache.

The bristly whiskers didn't cooperate. "Don't they know I can't fix a problem if I don't know about it?"

"I'm really sorry to hear Lynell may be . . ." *Slipping* was the word that came to mind. "I haven't talked to him lately, but he's always seemed so sharp. You know he does the crossword puzzle in the paper every week and does it in record time."

William humphed in a derisive way. "That doesn't do me any good if he forgets to deliver the paper to a whole block-full of subscribers."

"No, I suppose not."

"Well, don't you worry, Abby. I'll figure out if he's lying to me or just plain forgetful. You'll get your paper next week, I promise you that. And get it on time too." With that, he marched out the door as though on a mission to track down the miscreant who had failed in his duty to the *Birdcall*.

Worried about Lynell's mental health, Abby shook her head before turning back to Henry, who still looked a bit shell-shocked by the crowd of complaining residents.

"If you have a minute, I'd like to talk to you," she said to him.

"I hope you're not here about the robberies."

"I am, actually. But not to complain. I think I may have a lead for you."

He ran his palm over the top of his balding head. "I could sure use a decent lead right about now. Come on back to my office."

Letting her go first, Henry ushered Abby down the hall toward his office. Most Wanted posters were tacked up on cork-board on one side of the hallway and there were civil service announcements on the other.

Henry took the chair behind his metal desk while she sat down opposite him. She put Opal's audiotape on his desk.

"As you know, Mary's been receiving a series of hang-up

phone calls, which I suspect are from the thief. He's checking to see if anyone is at home. That first time he was surprised because she didn't get to the phone in time to answer it while he was on the line."

Nodding, Henry loosened his tie and undid the top button of his shirt. Abby suspected the scene out front with a mob of angry residents had created a lot of stress. She felt sorry about that. Henry was too good a man and police officer to be browbeaten for not immediately catching a wily thief.

"Go on," he said.

"So I decided to find out if any of the other victims had received phone calls like that. The Blackstocks have gotten some calls, but at least some of those were crank calls from three sixth graders who were just fooling around. Belinda Brisbin's going to get back to me after she checks with her husband and daughter. But I think I hit the jackpot with Opal Collins." She slid the tape toward Henry. "The Tuesday before her break-in she got one of those hang-up calls, except her answering machine picked up the call. She hadn't erased the message. The caller didn't say anything, but there's some background noise and you can hear him cough."

Henry raised his brows. "What makes you so sure it's our thief?"

"The timing's right and calling to check if anyone is home is part of his pattern."

Picking up the tape, Henry turned it over and studied the small device.

"I'm thinking if you can enhance the background noise, we can at least tell where he was when he made that call," Abby said. "Maybe someone spotted him loitering nearby."

"No caller ID on Opal's phone?"

"Afraid not."

"Which might not help anyway. Mary's last call turned out to be from a cloned phone with a Toledo area code. No way to tell where the call really came from or who made it."

"Did you question the two suspects I came up with?"

"I did. Darren Barber is an ex-con, but his parole officer says he's been playing it straight. He's been working steadily for the construction outfit down at the marina for about four months."

"He didn't have an alibi for a couple of the break-ins."

"He claimed he was just hanging out around town. I asked to see his cell phone. He gave it over without a fuss. The number didn't match either of the numbers we've got." He picked up a file folder that was lying next to his computer. "The other guy, Michael Romo, is a county employee but not a very good one. Bad absentee record. He's on probation and will probably get canned if he messes up again."

"Does he have a criminal record?"

"Nope. He's clean except for a couple of speeding tickets. He claims not to have a cell phone. Too expensive."

"Nowadays, it's hard to imagine a young person without their own phone."

"Maybe so, but I didn't have probable cause to pat him down."

Disappointed that Henry's questioning of the two men hadn't revealed anything new, Abby said, "Do you know if either Darren or Michael is a smoker? Or if they've had a bad cold recently?"

"What's that got to do with anything?"

"It's on the tape. The caller has a really bad cough."

Henry picked up the tape again. "Mike's my technical guy. Let's see what he can do with this."

A back room at the station house held an array of electronic equipment. At Henry's request, Mike pulled up a chair in front of a console and threw a switch. Dials and meters lit up. Taking the tape, he slid it into the machine.

"What are we looking for?" he asked. A tall, slender man in his thirties, Mike wore his hair in a short, military style.

"It's the second message on the tape," Abby explained. "I couldn't make out what the background noise is. I'm hoping you can enhance the sound."

Mike checked with his boss, who nodded his approval.

They listened to the message about the cultural arts meeting. Then came the suspicious call. At the end of the call, Mike stopped the tape.

"That's the one you want?"

"Do your magic," Henry said.

As he played the tape this time, Mike fussed with some dials until a black squiggly line appeared on a green oscilloscope monitor. "Okay, I've tried to bring out the background noise. Let's see what we've got."

Abby listened carefully. The roar of a motor. High-pitched voices.

"Those are children's voices," she concluded.

Henry agreed. "What's that first part?"

After another adjustment, Mike played the tape again. "I'd say it was an engine. Probably a truck, is my guess."

"That's not real helpful," Henry said. "The guy could be calling from anywhere on the island. Or even off-island somewhere."

"No, if that's our robber, he'd be close to Opal's house so he could break in right away if no one's at home."

But what kind of a truck? One that wouldn't be out of place in the neighborhood. Could a UPS truck be passing by? Or a delivery truck?

Abby thought back to her conversations with Opal as Mike played the tape one more time.

"A school bus!" she exclaimed. "Opal said the school bus stop is just a couple of houses up the street from hers. And those voices of children are the ones who got off the bus at that stop."

Henry grinned at her. "You're good, Abby. You sure you don't want to join the sheriff's department? I hear the residents are raising a fuss to get more deputies assigned to Sparrow Island."

She laughed and shook her head. "I'm happy with the job I have, thanks." Carrying a gun held little appeal for her.

"Let me know if you change your mind." Henry patted Mike's shoulder by way of thanking him. "Guess I'm going to go have a talk with the school bus driver. See if she can remember seeing anything out of the ordinary that day."

Abby didn't have to think twice. "I'll go with you. We both need to solve this case as soon as possible."

CHAPTER ❧ EIGHT

$\mathbb{A}$BBY WALKED FROM THE
sheriff's office across the street to the school with Henry. The
school bus and Mollie Berman, the driver, were in the school
parking lot waiting for the dismissal bell to ring. Leaning
against the front fender, Mollie was listening to music on an
iPod, tapping her foot to the beat.

"Hey, Mollie." Henry touched the brim of his hat. "Have
you got a few minutes?"

A woman in her forties who loved children and had three
of her own, Mollie pulled out the ear pieces and smiled. "My
kids gave this to me for Christmas and taught me how to
download whatever music I want to listen to. It's been great.
Now I can tune them out like they've been tuning me out for
years."

She laughed and glanced curiously from Henry to Abby
and back again. She wore heavy denim slacks and a khaki
jacket over a cotton blouse.

"What can I do for you, Sergeant?"

"I assume you've heard about the recent break-ins we've had on the island," Henry said.

"Oh sure. Even the kids have been talking about the robberies. Some of the younger ones are kinda scared hearing about it. I have to hush up the older boys when they start making the break-ins sound too gruesome." She shrugged. "You know how kids try to scare each other."

"I suppose I do," Henry said. "We're trying to get a lead on who's doing the break-ins. There's reason to believe he may have been somewhere near Opal Collins' house off Primrose Lane a week ago last Tuesday at about the time the school bus went by that afternoon. It's possible you may have seen him."

"Oh golly. I don't know. . . ." She scrunched her round face into a picture of concentration, which turned her eyes into narrow slits. "You say a week ago Tuesday? In the afternoon."

"You might have seen him walking along the street, probably wearing a dark jacket or shirt," Abby suggested. "Or he might have been in a truck of some sort."

"That was the week my Stevie was sick and I had to leave him with a neighbor. Let me think." She slid her hands in her jacket pocket and pulled out a key ring. She jiggled the keys in her hand as if that might help her recall the day in question. "I usually see the UPS truck sometime on my route. Driver's a nice guy. He waves, but I don't know his name."

Both Abby and Henry remained silent, letting Mollie recall what she could.

"A couple of times that week I had to let the kids off at a different stop because they were putting new asphalt on the streets on that side of the island."

"Yes, they've been trying to resurface a lot of our streets before the summer rush," Abby said.

"I don't remember anyone on foot except parents meeting the bus to pick up their kids, but I think I saw a telephone company truck." She put the keys back in her pocket. "I'm not sure whether that was Tuesday or Wednesday though. I didn't pay much attention."

"Okay. Anything else?" Henry asked.

She shook her head. "Nothing comes to mind."

"We think these robberies are occurring during the late afternoon," Henry told her. "Since you're out driving around at that time of day, keep an eye out for anyone you think is suspicious or out of place." Henry handed her one of his business cards.

"I will. Golly, I sure hope you catch him."

"We're all praying for that," Abby said wholeheartedly. She reached into her pocket and pulled out a business card as well. She jotted her cell phone number on the back, a number she rarely gave out. "If you do see anything unusual, don't hesitate to call either me or the sheriff's substation."

Mollie examined both cards, then dropped them in her jacket pocket. "Sure, I'll call. I really hate it that someone's stealing from our own people."

The school bell sounded, and Mollie pulled out her keys again. "Here come my little darlin's now. Through rain and snow and sleet, I'll see 'em home safe." With that, she climbed into the bus and settled herself in the driver's seat. "I'll keep a sharp eye out, you can be sure of that."

Henry touched the brim of his hat again, then he and Abby stepped away from the bus. Just in time, too, as the first of

Mollie's young riders came blasting out of the school building, yelling and screaming as they raced to be first on the bus.

"You have to give credit to anyone who enjoys children as much as Mollie does," Abby commented.

"The school district's lucky to have her."

Dodging children, they strolled back toward the sheriff's substation.

"What now?" Abby asked.

"I think I'll check with the phone company. First I'll find out if they had a truck over here on that Tuesday. Then I'll see if they can give me a list of phone numbers that placed calls to Opal's house last week."

"Will you let me know what you find out?"

"Sure. In fact, Mary invited me to dinner tonight. If I've learned anything by then, I'll let you know."

MARY SET COLORFUL LINEN PLACE MATS and matching napkins on the dining room table for dinner, then returned to the kitchen to get the silver place settings. She didn't often do large dinner parties, as she had when Jacob was alive. But she still enjoyed setting a nice table, even for informal occasions.

She found her low crystal candleholders and a pair of lavender-scented tapers that would go nicely with the place mats.

Back in the kitchen, she asked Finnegan to open the refrigerator door, which he did by pulling on a leather strap attached to the handle.

"Good boy," she said, taking the marinated sirloin steak strips out of the refrigerator for grilling and putting them on the counter. She checked the oven to see that the baked potatoes were nearly done. Henry was a big man and expended a lot of calories on his job. She worried that he didn't eat well enough when he was on his own.

"Mary Reynolds!" Laughing, she chided herself out loud. "Henry has been taking care of himself just fine without your help."

True, but she did love to cook for others. Apparently old habits die hard.

The doorbell rang, and she felt a spurt of excitement as she went to answer the door. Finnegan trotted along beside her. She found Henry standing on the front porch holding a bouquet of flowers. He'd changed out of his uniform and was wearing slacks, a sport shirt and a tan windbreaker.

"Pretty flowers for a pretty lady," he said.

"Oh, aren't you sweet."

He put the flowers in her arms and kissed her lightly on her lips. "I stopped by Island Blooms. Candace says you haven't been in all week."

Wheeling back from the door, she sniffed the fragrant scent of the mixed bouquet. "I've been staying home in case that thief tries again, but I have to go to the shop tomorrow to pay bills. Besides, I'm going stir-crazy here all day."

Chuckling, Henry closed the door behind him.

"Come help me put these in a vase," she said. "They'll look lovely on the table tonight. Abby should be home soon."

Gripping the handles on the wheelchair, Henry pushed her into the kitchen.

"Are you having any luck identifying our thief?" She pointed to a high cupboard. "The vases are up there."

"Nothing but dead ends, so far." He selected a ceramic vase with a bright floral motif.

Nodding her approval, Mary found a pair of scissors in a drawer and began snipping the flowers to the suitable length for the arrangement she had in mind. "I'm sure you'll break the case soon."

"I'd better." He leaned back against the counter and watched her work. "The townspeople are really on my case. I had a near riot in my office this afternoon."

"Oh dear. I'm sorry to hear that."

"I understand why they're upset, but they've got to give me a chance to do my job. Archie has called a town council meeting for tomorrow night and he's ordered me to report our progress."

"He can get pretty pushy sometimes." She snipped purple statice to length, arranged them in the vase, and added a pair of daffodils. Candace had put together a well-blended assortment for her. As always. The young woman had been a godsend at the shop since Mary's accident and lived up to her role as manager.

"Come to think of it, they're going to be publicizing the council meeting all around town. I'd like you to be there."

She looked up at him. "To cheer for you?"

He smiled crookedly. "That'd be nice. But I'm thinking our thief just might want to know what's going on. What clues we're working on and how the investigation's going. If he's there, you might be able to pick him out of the crowd."

"Oh, I don't know." She leaned back in her chair. "I got such a short glimpse of him. Though I doubt I'll ever forget what he looked like from the rear. Dark hair that was a little shaggy. He moved fast when he realized I was at home."

"And had a dog," Henry added.

"That too." She sent a grateful smile toward Finnegan, who had curled up out of the way near the kitchen table. "I had the sense the thief was fairly young, no older than about thirty."

"I'll have one of my deputies stay with you in the back of the room. If you see someone you think might be our guy, the deputy can talk to him, get his ID."

"I'm certainly happy to help if I can." Studying the final floral arrangement, she made a couple of adjustments and decided the result suited her. "Would you put these on the table for me, please?"

"Happy to."

A few minutes later, Abby arrived home. While she went upstairs to freshen up, Mary started the steaks on the countertop electric grill and Henry delivered the salad and condiments to the table, and poured their water.

When Abby came downstairs, she commented, "Goodness, you two make a good team. Everything looks lovely and smells wonderful. Is there anything left I can help with?"

"Not a thing," Mary said. "I think we're ready to sit, if you are."

"Perfect. I'm starved. I forgot to eat lunch today. All I had were a few crackers and cheese from the museum's store of snacks."

Henry took his place at the head of the table, Mary and Abby sitting opposite each other.

"If I may, I'd like to say grace tonight." Mary bowed her head. "Dear Lord, thank You for the food we eat and the blessings of friendship and love at this table. Please help Henry to solve his case and catch the thief who has shaken our sense of security. And keep us all safe. We ask this in Your name. Amen."

"Amen," Henry and Abby echoed in determined voices.

As they ate, they chatted about general news around the island—the weather, ferry employees threatening to go out on strike, a resident of Friday Harbor who got lost on his boat and had to be towed back home.

As Henry was finishing the last of his steak, Abby ventured the question that was on her mind. "Did you make that call to the phone company?"

Putting down his fork, he took a sip of water before responding. "I did. The telephone company tells me they have a repairman assigned to Sparrow Island two or three days a week. They have to check to see if one was here the Tuesday of Opal's break-in. They'll get back to me."

Abby nodded, waiting for him to continue.

"The business office faxed me a list of all the calls that connected to Opal's home phone. The Toledo number popped up on the list twice, including the day she was robbed."

"Then that confirms he's our thief," Abby said.

"Whoever *he* is, which we can't figure out until we find the cloned phone itself."

"What about the Washington area code that called me?" Mary asked.

"It didn't show up on Opal's list." He pushed his plate aside and folded his napkin beside it. "I've asked the phone company to check calls to your phone and to all the homes that have been robbed."

"Be sure you include the Brisbins in that list," Abby said. "Belinda called me this afternoon at the museum. Her daughter remembered getting a call from someone who hung up as soon as she answered the phone. She thought it might've been a boy who got cold feet at the last minute and hung up. But I'm guessing it was our thief."

"Yep, I gave the Brisbins' number to the phone company too."

"But the bottom line is we're no further along than we were this afternoon." Discouraged, Abby set her napkin aside too. "Since the phone numbers aren't getting us anywhere, we have to think of some other way to approach the case."

"True," Henry agreed. "Unfortunately, my gray matter hasn't come up with another angle to follow."

"What I'd like to know," Mary said, "is why the thief is targeting my house. What's he after here?"

Abby mentally inventoried the house. When she remodeled the downstairs, she'd moved Mary's belongings into her new bedroom. She hadn't come across anything of noteworthy value. The kitchen had been the most complicated part of the job, but Jacob's collection of scrimshaw had required the most care. She'd been terrified the workmen would damage the oak and glass case in which they were displayed.

Abruptly, Abby stood, picked up her plate and Henry's, carrying them into the kitchen, then returned for Mary's.

"What do you think Jacob's scrimshaw is worth?" she asked.

"Oh, I don't know. He was very proud of his collection. Some of the pieces are quite old. Some were carved by whalers and others by Native Americans. Others he had carved himself and were quite special to him."

"What are you getting at, Abby?" Henry asked.

She held up one finger to hold off his question. "Is the scrimshaw collection insured?"

"Why, yes." Tilting her head to one side, Mary considered

the question. "The collection is covered on my homeowner's insurance. Jacob added that years ago, and I've simply continued to pay the additional charges."

Still holding Mary's empty plate, Abby sat down in her chair again. "Who's your insurance agent?"

"Originally, Adam Billings sold us the policy. But now Tucker handles all of my insurance for both the house and my van."

"That's it!" Snatching up the salad bowl, she carried that and Mary's plate into the kitchen.

"Wait! What's *it*?" Henry asked. "I'm not following you."

She returned to the dining room. "Wilma Washburn had the cedar mask that was stolen covered on her homeowner's policy. Margaret Blackstock complained about all the insurance forms she had to fill out to prove the value of the painting and an Indian basket that were taken. Brenda and Kyle Wilson lost a Salish Indian mask, and I'm betting it was insured. I'll almost guarantee Opal Wilson's silver tea and coffee service were insured too." She picked up their drinking glasses. "Tucker's the only independent insurance agent in town. Maybe not everyone on Sparrow Island goes to him for their insurance needs, but I'll bet he has a pretty big share of the market."

"He, and his father before him, always got me the best price available. I've always trusted him," Mary said.

"I don't think Abby's necessarily saying that Tucker's behind these robberies. But he could be the common thread between them."

"And how the robber knows which houses will be worth his while to break into." Pensive, Abby stood holding the water glasses in her hands. "I wonder if we can find a connection between Tucker Billings and Michael Romo or Darren Barber, the workmen I identified as not having an alibi for some of the robberies."

"I guess I'll try to find out tomorrow." Henry set his jaw in determination.

Abby did the same. She had some questions she wanted to ask Sparrow Island's most popular insurance agent.

CHAPTER ✿ NINE

T UCKER BILLINGS' OFFICE
was in a modest house in an older residential neighborhood
up the hill from Municipal Street. It had been the first home
of the senior Billingses when they arrived in Sparrow Island in
the 1960s. As Adam's insurance business prospered, the young
family moved to a larger home with an ocean view and con-
verted the cottage to commercial use.

A little after nine o'clock in the morning, Abby met Henry
on the sidewalk in front of the house. While Henry generally
thought police work should be left to him and his deputies, he
couldn't deny that Abby had a nose for detective work. If
Henry felt there was no physical danger involved he would
reluctantly let Abby join him when gathering information.

"Did you call to make sure he was in?" she asked.

Henry squared his campaign hat on his head. "I prefer to
drop by unannounced. You never know what someone will say
or how they'll act when you catch them off guard."

Good strategy, she thought with a smile.

Well-manicured flower beds bright with petunias and pansies lined both sides of the brick-colored walkway to the porch. A tasteful bronze plaque on the white door announced they had arrived at Billings & Billings Insurance Services. Opening the door, Henry allowed Abby to enter first.

Lush forest-green carpeting covered the reception area and a young woman in her twenties sat behind a walnut desk. Hitting a few last keystrokes on her computer, she turned to greet them. The nameplate on the desk read Jade Kebby.

"Good morning," she said brightly. "May I help you?"

Henry removed his hat. "We'd like to speak to Mr. Billings. Is he in?"

"Is he expecting you?"

"We won't take up much of his time."

Her brown-eyed gaze flicked to the multiple-line phone on her desk. "Let me see if he's busy. Who should I say—"

Henry provided their names, including his rank as sergeant.

Gracefully, she came to her feet and walked to the nearby open door. Fairly tall with dark, curly hair, she wore a long cotton skirt that came to her calves in a swirl of colors, sandals and a silky turquoise blouse with a neckline that plunged a little more than necessary.

As she stepped out of sight into her boss's office, Henry said under his breath, "Secretaries are getting younger every day."

"I suspect it's because we're getting older."

He grunted noncommittally.

Jade reappeared. "Mr. Billings will see you now." She stood back so they could enter. "Would you like some coffee? Anything?"

"We're fine," Abby told her. "Thanks."

Tucker met them on the visitors' side of his large mahogany

desk. Extending his hand first to Abby and then to Henry, he said, "Abby, it's good to see you. And you, Sergeant Cobb. What brings you here this morning?"

"We're investigating the robberies we've been having lately," Henry said.

Tucker's usual pleasant expression clouded. "There has been a regular plague of thefts lately, hasn't there?" He gestured toward a conversational grouping of upholstered chairs by a window that looked out onto a well-kept backyard. He was almost as tall as Henry, but somewhat thinner with a narrow face and thinning black hair. Abby thought he was in his early forties, although he might be a little younger than that. As she recalled, he was still single.

She took the chair closest to the window. Henry sat next to her and Tucker sat down opposite them, on the other side of a glass-topped coffee table. Insurance brochures of various sorts were carefully arranged on the table.

"I'm not sure how I can help you, Sergeant, but I'm happy to try." Settling back in his chair, Tucker unbuttoned his suit jacket and appeared completely relaxed. And innocent of any wrongdoing.

"I understand some of the victims had their stolen items insured by you," Henry said.

"We wrote the homeowner policies for them, true. But there were a couple of different companies involved. I make it a point to shop around for the best deals I can make for my clients. Sometimes there are small differences between coverages and deductibles."

"In the past few weeks, there have been five robberies," Abby said. She did not mention the attempt at Mary's house, who was also insured via Billings. "Did you write the insurance on all five homes?"

Tucker seemed to mentally count the recent claims. "That's correct. We've been working with our clients to process their claims to make sure they get what's due them in an expeditious manner. Both my secretary and I have been kept busy staying on top of the problem. Our clients come first, you know."

Henry leaned forward, his elbows resting on his thighs, his hat dangling from his fingers. "Do you find it unusual that all five household that were robbed were insured by you?"

"Not at all. Regrettable, of course. But over the years both my father and I have built up a reputation in the community for providing good service and individual attention to our clients. While we may not represent *all* of the local homeowners, I expect we've written a good percentage of the insurance coverage on the island." The corners of his narrow lips lifted into a smile. "Lately, I've been expanding our services to the other islands. I don't mind going head-to-head with the brokers at Friday Harbor, I'll tell you that."

"Commendable," Henry said, though not with a lot of feeling. "Tucker, could we take a look at the claims your clients have filed? I'd like to compare them with what they reported stolen to our office."

Tucker's mobile expression darkened again. "Sergeant, I consider our files confidential. Without my clients' permission, I'm reluctant to release—"

"We could get a court order, but that would take time." Henry held Tucker in a steady gaze. "I'm sure you agree we need to identify the thief as quickly as possible. A delay might mean another of your clients suffers a loss. I'm sure neither you nor the companies that underwrite your policies would like that to happen."

"Of course not." Tucker stood and buttoned his jacket again. The suit fit him well, as though it had been hand tailored, and the fabric looked expensive—a medium gray with a maroon thread running through it that matched his silk tie. "I'll ask Jade to pull the files for you. It will just take a few moments."

After Tucker had left the room, Abby said, "He doesn't act like he has anything to hide."

"He works at being honest and trustworthy, and it looks like he's got a pretty successful business going. Hard to see his motivation for being involved in a string of robberies of his own clients."

Abby agreed, which meant Tucker wasn't a suspect. But the insurance angle still provided a connection between the break-ins.

Tucker returned with a handful of files neatly arranged and labeled in manila folders. "These are the five claims we're processing. I appreciate that your police reports are public record, but I'd like you to treat this information as confidential."

"Of course." Henry took the folders and handed the top one to Abby. "Besides you and your secretary, who has access to your files?"

"No one. We lock them up every night before we go home, and the building has an alarm system. We'd know if someone had broken in and tampered with the files." Tucker sat down and unbuttoned his jacket again. "As I say, we take our responsibilities to our clients very seriously."

Abby read through the details of Margaret Blackstock's claim. She found no surprises in the report.

Putting that file on the table, she picked up the claim file for Belinda Brisbin next. Nothing jumped out at her in that report either, except an ancient stone maul for grinding seeds was mentioned as well as a woven cedar hat. There was a picture of both. They were valued at seven hundred dollars.

"Henry, did the police report filed by the Brisbins mention a couple of Indian artifacts?"

He glanced up from his reading. "I don't recall. I remember Wilma was particularly concerned about some sort of a mask. A family heirloom."

"Yes, the loss of that mask was a real tragedy for her," Tucker said. "I sincerely hope you're able to recover the mask and restore it to her."

"That's what we're working on," Henry said, returning to his reading.

Belinda Brisbin's file produced no other new information. But when Abby opened Opal Collins' file she found a picture of several small white bones displayed on a blue velvet background. As she read through the report, she identified the bones as a sla-hal game, valued at two thousand dollars.

"Wow!" she said. "I don't know what a sla-hal game is or how to play it, but it's worth a lot more than my family's Monopoly set."

"Yes, indeed. Ms. Collins had a real find in that." Reaching across the table, Tucker picked up the snapshot of the bones. "It's an unusual game played with thirteen bones, although it's not clear to me what kind of bones. Several Northwestern Native American groups had similar games. They involve a degree of spirituality, competition and some guesswork."

"A dice game?" Henry asked.

"I'd say more than that, with some religious element or foretelling the future."

Leaning back in the chair, Abby looked out into the backyard and considered the fact that all of the victims had lost at least one valuable artifact. She watched as a half-dozen Savannah sparrows flitted in and out of a blackberry bush along the back fence. It wasn't unusual for people of the Northwest to have collections of Native American artifacts. After all, Native Americans lived here long before other people settled the land.

But was it reasonable that *every* break-in resulted in the theft of that kind of a valuable collector's item?

She turned back to Tucker. "What percentage of your clients would you say have special insurance coverage for a collection of Indian artifacts?"

"Why, I don't know." He appeared surprised by her question. "I suppose half the people in the islands have an arrowhead stashed away somewhere, but they're not valuable enough to insure."

"What about the more valuable collections?" she persisted.

Henry was paying close attention too. "That's a good question, Tucker. Abby may be on to something."

Tucker gave that some thought. "Museum quality pieces? I'd say I've written riders that cover no more than thirty items, although there may be more than that on the islands, but covered through an agent other than myself."

"Have the artifacts gone up in value lately?" Henry questioned.

"I'm not an expert, you understand. But I do ask the owners to have them reappraised periodically and provide me with the documentation."

"Do they do it?" Abby asked.

He shrugged. "Probably not as often as they should."

Abby vowed to ask Mary to get her scrimshaw collection evaluated by an expert. It could well be more valuable than she realized. She was glad that the artifacts at the Nature Museum were insured by an organization that specialized in museum pieces.

Henry pressed on with Tucker. "But you are saying that five out of thirty of your clients with collections of artifacts have been robbed lately."

Tucker's complexion darkened. "Are you implying—"

"I'm not implying anything. I'm simply trying to get a handle on these robberies. In my business, coincidences make me nervous. It's entirely possible that it's more than random chance that only your clients have been victims."

"So far," Tucker added.

Placing the files in the center of the coffee table, Henry stood. So did Abby and Tucker.

"Could you get me a list of all of your clients who have these special riders on their policies?" Henry said.

Looking decidedly less friendly than when they'd arrived, Tucker agreed. "It will take some time. My secretary will have to go through the records of several hundred clients."

"I understand. In the next day or so would be helpful." Extending his hand, Henry thanked Tucker for seeing them without an appointment.

Abby thanked him as well and started to leave, but stopped before she got to the office door. "There's one other thing. Do you happen to know either Darren Barber or Michael Romo?"

Tucker's eyebrows lowered. "The names don't sound familiar. Who are they?"

"Two young men in their twenties. They've been working here on the island recently."

Shaking his head and smiling, he said, "My secretary would be far more likely to be acquainted with them than I am. She appears to have quite a string of admirers."

"I see." But to Abby's regret, Jade wasn't at her desk as they left. According to Tucker, his secretary had asked permission to run an errand in town and wouldn't be back until after lunch.

Abby decided the girl would be worth talking to later. Maybe the thief was getting access to the files through her.

As they reached the sidewalk, Henry said, "Your brain seemed to be working on overdrive in there."

A cool breeze had picked up, and her hair fluttered across her face. She brushed the strands back where they belonged. "I have the feeling the thief is specifically after the artifacts. Whatever else he takes is a cover for that. As you told Tucker, it's too coincidental otherwise."

"If that's true, how is he getting rid of the goods? There can't be that big a market for cedar masks and games where you roll bones. Plus, their insurance value wasn't that high. Two thousand dollars max. Hardly a big take for the risk involved."

Except the thief hadn't been taking much of a risk. He'd known exactly which houses to break into and took care that the owners weren't at home.

"First thing I'm going to do is get Mary to have an expert reappraise her scrimshaw collection for insurance purposes," Abby said. "Maybe the expert will know what the market is like and whether the values have risen lately."

"Sounds like a plan." He stopped beside his police cruiser.

"Let me know what you find out. Meanwhile, I'm going do a little digging into Tucker's finances and his secretary's social life."

"Are you going to warn the people at the town council meeting tonight to be extra cautious if they own Indian artifacts?"

He contemplated his answer for several moments before responding. "I'm afraid that would tip our hand to the thief. It might spook him altogether and make it that much harder to recover what's already been stolen."

"I see your point." But she was also glad that she'd be able to warn Mary privately about her collection.

"When I get the whole list of Tucker's clients who own artifacts, I may make some discrete calls on the families and suggest they put their valuables in a safety deposit box. At least temporarily."

ABBY AND MARY ARRIVED at the town council meeting early. Even so, a large crowd had already gathered. Apparently an official notice in the *Birdcall* wasn't needed to spread the word in the community.

Tables and five chairs for the council members had been placed on risers at one end of the Community Center hall. Folding chairs were arranged in rows for the audience, and a portable podium was placed off to the side for those who wished to speak to the council, or—like Henry—had been ordered to report to the community.

Abby pushed Mary's wheelchair toward the center aisle.

"Henry suggested I stay toward the back of the audience," Mary said. "Since I only saw the thief from the back, I'll have to try to identify him from that angle."

"Maybe from the way he walks or his hair?" She pulled Mary toward the back wall. Finnegan reversed his course as well.

"I'm not very optimistic," Mary admitted.

Abby stood talking with her sister, watching the new arrivals and wondering if the thief would actually show up, or if he did, whether Mary would be able to identify the man.

They hadn't been there long when Deputy Mike Bennett arrived.

"Ladies." He acknowledged both Mary and Abby with a nod. "The sarge asked me to stay close to you in case you see the man who broke into your house."

"I'll do the best I can," Mary told him.

The deputy took up a position to the left of Mary while Finnegan guarded her opposite side.

When Abby scanned the room again, she spotted Dorthea Gilmore, the infamous donut police of Men's Club fame, enter and find a seat off to the side of the room. Curious, Abby excused herself from Mary, who was visiting with her friend Ana Dominguez. Ana was a member of the town council and owner of In Stitches, the source of much of Mary's yarn and craft supplies.

"I'll be back in a minute," she told Mary.

She made her way across the room to where Ms. Gilmore was sitting alone. Since she didn't think the woman had been on Sparrow Island or even in the San Juans long, Abby found it interesting that she would attend this meeting. But then, if she was assigned here temporarily, maybe she thought this would be a way to meet some of the residents.

"Hello. You're Dorthea Gilmore, aren't you?"

The woman glanced up in surprise and stood. Dressed in a

tailored pants suit, she was slightly taller than Abby's five feet five, with short, dark hair and a figure that was almost boyishly slender. She wore only a trace of lip gloss. Up close, she appeared somewhat younger than Abby had guessed. Perhaps in her late thirties.

"I am Ms. Gilmore. Do I know you?"

"No, but I believe you know my father. I'm Abby Stanton, George Stanton's daughter."

Recognition sparked in her hazel eyes. "I see. If you're here to lobby on his behalf, then I must tell you I'm working on orders from the governor. Obesity is a major problem in our state—"

"Oh, no, it's not that. It's simply that I know you're new to the island, and I wanted to extend a friendly welcome."

"Oh, well . . . thank you." She looked taken aback by Abby's welcome. "Would you like to sit? . . ." She made a vague gesture toward the chair next to hers.

"No, I'm here with my sister, who's sitting in the back. I admit, after seeing you at one of the protests, I was a bit curious."

"About the officious government bureaucrat who's denying donuts to elderly men who ought to take better care of their health?"

Abby felt the heat of embarrassment color her cheeks. She had been thinking something along those lines and chided herself for her unkind thoughts.

"I get the feeling yours is not an easy job," she said. "I'm truly sorry your assignment here in Green Harbor has made you uncomfortable. I'm sure you and the Men's Club will eventually come to an agreement."

Once again Dorthea appeared surprised. "You really think so?"

"I think change is hard for everyone." She tried for her friendliest smile. "You'll have to excuse me, but I have to get back to my sister."

As she walked back across the room, she noticed Deputy Bennett still hovered near Mary, his attention on the audience that had gathered. She pulled up a chair next to her sister.

"Anyone look familiar?" she asked.

"I'm afraid I'm not very good at identifying anyone by their rear ends. I picked out one kid wearing jeans. When he turned around, I realized it was Bobby! That child is growing up too fast."

Abby chuckled and looked up as Archie Goodfellow pounded a gavel to bring the meeting to order. In addition to Archie and Ana Dominguez, who'd taken her seat on the risers, the other members of the council had arrived—Frank Holloway, owner of the hardware store, Ed Willoughby, who owned the drugstore, and Keith Gordon, a man with a lovely Scottish brogue who owned the Dorset.

After describing the series of robberies that had happened on the island, Archie called Henry to the podium to give a report on his progress.

He spoke briefly, and to the dismay of most of the people in the audience, his message was pretty much as it had been yesterday—he and his deputies were doing everything they could to bring the criminal to justice and recover the stolen merchandise.

Meanwhile, Abby scanned the audience in search of Darren Barber or Michael Romo. Or Jade, for that matter. None of her prime suspects were present, although she recognized many of her friends and neighbors from the community, including the crime victims.

"What's taking you so long to arrest someone?" some disgruntled man in the audience asked Henry.

"I don't want to go into specifics of an ongoing investigation," Henry explained with more patience than the man deserved. "But I assure you, we are making progress."

"If it were me, I'd have the guy hogtied and keelhauled by now," another man grumbled.

A murmur of agreement rippled through the crowd.

"I understand you're all upset," Henry said. "But what we don't need are people taking the law into their own hands."

"In the old days, we had vigilantes, and they got the job done!"

Henry visibly winced at that suggestion. "For now, I'd urge you all to keep your doors locked and your valuables in a safe place."

A woman jumped to her feet. "Then you're saying the sheriff's office can't protect our property."

"Ma'am, we're doing—"

Archie pounded his gavel. "Hang on a minute. Ana's got an idea. Let her talk."

In her quiet way, Ana waited for the crowd to simmer down, then spoke softly in her lightly accented voice that still held traces of her birthplace in Mexico. "Sergeant Cobb is a good man and is doing his job. But we are all neighbors and we can help the most by watching out for each other and our homes. We can watch for strangers in our neighborhoods and call the sheriff's office if we see something suspicious. We are our own best protection against thieves and criminals."

"We had a Neighborhood Watch in Tacoma where we come from," a woman said.

Ana nodded. "*Sí*, that is what I mean. We watch out for each other."

"I got a lot of nosy neighbors who'd be good at that," a man said loudly enough for everyone to hear but without identifying himself.

Everyone chuckled, and the tension that had been in the air seemed to ease. Abby had always been amazed that Ana, a businesswoman and the token female on the council, had the ability to bring a group together, while the men often wanted to continue to argue.

Henry spoke up. "I'd like to see us organize a Neighborhood Watch here on Sparrow Island. It's a very successful program in many communities, and I'm sure it would be here too. It takes a while to put a good program together, and I'd be happy to help do that, but for now I think Ana has the right idea. We all keep an eye out for each other."

We are our brother's keeper, Abby thought.

The meeting ended on that reasonably optimistic note, despite Mary's disappointment that she'd failed to identify the robber.

"You're right not to finger someone if you're not sure, ma'am," Deputy Bennett assured her.

As Abby pushed Mary toward the exit, she spotted Dorthea Gilmore walking out with Tucker Billings, who was smiling down at his companion.

Abby mentally did a double take. They made an unlikely couple, Tucker so upbeat and Dorthea so regimented in her thinking.

Had they simply been sitting together and made a friendly connection? Or had they arranged to meet here?

Returning her attention to getting Mary through the crowd without running over anyone's toes, she told herself whatever the relationship between Dorthea and Tucker, it was none of her business.

CHAPTER 🌹 TEN

T HE FOLLOWING MORNING, Mary took Abby's advice to heart. She placed a call to Richard Decker in Seattle. A well-respected dealer of scrimshaw and other artifacts, his expertise had helped Jacob build his scrimshaw collection without being duped by those who tried to pass off modern replicas for the real thing.

"You're wise to have your collection reappraised," he told her over the phone. "There's been an increasing interest recently in Native American products of all sorts."

"Then you'd say that I may have to increase my insurance coverage to reflect current values?"

"No question about it. I have some clients who have switched a significant portion of their investments to antiquities of all sorts. That shift has definitely driven up the value."

Fortunately, Richard was available to come to Sparrow Island the next day and would arrive in the afternoon. Mary said she'd look forward to seeing him.

When she hung up, she wheeled into the living room and stopped in front of the oak and glass display cabinet Jacob had built. Finely drawn sailing vessels, northern landscapes, trees, birds and totems were carved into walrus tusks and whalebone. Each piece of art represented hours upon hours of hard work, dedication and artistic talent. A few examples dated back to the 1700s. Others were carved during the nineteenth century. Jacob valued each piece and so did Mary, especially the ones Jacob made himself.

"It would be a shame to lose a single piece of scrimshaw, much less the entire collection." Idly, she petted Finnegan, who had come to sit beside her. "No matter how much I increase the insurance, it wouldn't make up for what Jacob so lovingly collected and created."

But she was loathe to pack them all up and hide them away in some bank vault where neither she nor anyone else could enjoy them.

"Henry will simply have to catch the thief and do it soon!"

Wheeling toward the front hall, she got her jacket out of the closet and made her way to the garage.

Just as eager to get out of the house as she was, Finnegan trotted along beside her.

Thief or not, she had to go into Island Blooms. Fridays were one of the busiest days of the week in the flower business. She'd left Candace on her own since the attempted robbery. That wasn't fair to her shop manager. Furthermore, there were bills to be paid. Her suppliers depended on her as much as she relied on them.

But she'd make it a point to be back home by the afternoon, the time when the thief liked to strike. If and when he called to see if it was all clear to steal from her, she'd be there. And he'd stay away.

AS WAS HER CUSTOM, Mary parked behind Island Blooms and entered by the back door. The floral scent of roses, lisianthus, lilies, statice and daisy poms perfumed the workroom. Scattered about the worktable were rolls of ribbon, stacks of vases and other signs that Candace had been hard at work. A partially completed arrangement waited for her return.

Mary wheeled to the front of the store where she found Candace with a customer, a woman who Mary didn't recognize.

"If you change the water every couple of days, this arrangement should last almost a week," Candace said.

"They're lovely. I know my mother will be pleased. Thank you so much." With her purse slung over her shoulder, the woman picked up the arrangement and carried it out the front door.

Candace turned to see Mary. "I thought I heard you come in. I've missed you this week. And Finnegan too." As she knelt to give the dog a good scratch behind his ears, her waist-length strawberry-blonde hair almost touched the floor and her long skirt puddled around her feet.

"I decided I couldn't put my life on hold indefinitely because of the robber." Mary took a quick glance at the walk-in refrigerator where flowers were stored and decided the supply was adequate to take them through the weekend.

"I'm so sorry you had to experience that break-in. I'm glad you called to let me know what had happened. I understand why you wanted to stick close to home."

"From the signs in the workroom, it looks like you've been busy in my absence," Mary said.

"For a nonholiday period, we've done pretty well this week."

Mary rolled over to her desk. Without being told, Finnegan settled on the bit of carpeting under the desk where he'd be out of the way.

"Who was that woman who was just here?" she asked. "She looked familiar, but I can't place her."

"Ana Dominguez's daughter. She's visiting from Los Angeles for the weekend. I think it must be Ana's birthday."

"Oh, of course. I'd forgotten about Ana's birthday, though. I'll have to drop by with a card. Ana must be thrilled to have her girl here." Opening a side drawer, she withdrew the check register and the folder with current invoices to be paid. "No matter how grown up your children are, you miss seeing them when they move away." She certainly missed seeing her Zack and Nancy, and the grandchildren, of course.

"Say, have you heard about the open mic night they're going to have at Springhouse Café?"

Mary looked up from the invoices. "Don't tell me you're going to perform?"

Candace laughed. "Not me. But Brad's thinking about it."

"Is he going to tell lawyer jokes?" Candace's longtime boyfriend worked as an attorney in Seattle. On the surface, Candace, with her near-hippie lifestyle, and Brad, a more academic type, seemed to have little in common. But they appeared to have a loving relationship.

"He certainly knows a lot of them." She scrunched up her forehead in thought. "How about . . . How many lawyers does it take to change a lightbulb?"

Mary grimaced. "I don't know, dear. How many lawyers does it take?"

"It takes four. One to turn the bulb, one to round up

witnesses, one to push the first guy off the ladder, and one to file a class action suit against the ladder company."

Groaning, Mary shook her head. "You'd better tell him he'll have some stiff competition. I've been helping Bobby McDonald write jokes for his routine."

"You're going to perform?"

"No, no," she said in quick denial. "The jokes are for Bobby, not me."

Candace cocked her brow. "I think you ought to perform too. You'd be really funny."

Mary scowled at her. "No way!" Ironically, however, an odd assortment of jokes kept popping in her head at the most unexpected moments. She quickly shoved the thought aside. The fact that arranging flowers was like being an orchestra conductor with the world's limpest baton was *not* funny. "I'd better get these invoices paid or our suppliers will cut us off."

WHEN ABBY ARRIVED at the Nature Museum, she went directly to the exhibit area to check on the pupae display. The ballot box with visitors' guesses about what would emerge looked nearly full. But the pupae didn't seem to care. They remained as Bobby had found them, stuck to their respective cabbage leaves.

The weather had been improving daily. Abby had thought the warmth of spring would arouse the life inside the cocoons. Perhaps being in a building that remained the same temperature all day was slowing their cycle. She'd have to keep her eye out for butterflies and moths that were emerging in the neighbor's yard where Bobby had found the pupae.

She cocked her head to study the pupa on the lower leaf

more closely. Had the chrysalis changed just a little? Or was it her imagination?

She shook her head. She really ought to study up on insects, butterflies and moths in particular.

On the way to her office, she stopped by the reception desk, where she greeted Wilma.

"How are you feeling today?" she asked.

"Discouraged by Sergeant Cobb's lack of progress in getting my cedar mask back."

"Were you at the meeting last night?" Abby hadn't noticed her, although she'd been more intent on looking out for the couple of young men who had come under suspicion.

"For all the good it did me." From beneath the counter, Wilma pulled out a supply of conservatory self-guiding maps of the grounds and stacked them neatly together for visitors to pick up.

"Try not to be too disheartened. Henry's making more progress than he let on."

Wilma brightened at that. "Oh? Do you know something I don't?"

"Henry didn't want to reveal too much for fear he'd frighten the thief off before he got caught. But he's working on some leads." Abby intended to do the same as soon as she could get away from the office.

"I'd like to do more than just frighten the crook. I still feel sick to my stomach every time I think of losing my family's legacy."

She took Wilma's hand and squeezed it reassuringly. "I'll keep you in my prayers, Wilma. *And* your family's mask. I don't believe the Lord will fail you."

Wilma squeezed back. "I hope you're right."

In her office, Abby shed her jacket and hung it on the back of the door, then sat down to go through her mail. That accomplished, she turned on her computer to check her e-mail.

Hugo appeared at her doorway. "Knock knock," he said.

She looked up from the computer screen. "Come on in."

"No, Abby, you're supposed to say 'Who's there?'"

"Hugo, I know who you are. Come on . . ." She grimaced. "Oh, I get it. You're going to tell me one of your dreadful knock-knock jokes."

With mock offense, he drew himself up to his full five feet eleven inches, appearing even taller because his blue turtle neck sweater matched his twinkling eyes. "My jokes are, by definition, clever and witty."

"If you say so." She grinned at him.

"Very well. We'll start again. Knock knock."

She played along. "Who's there?"

"Ben."

"Ben who?"

"Ben wondering what you're up to!" He looked very proud of himself.

She stifled a groan.

"I could try another one," he suggested hopefully.

"No, that's all right. Why don't you save it for open mic night."

He sat down in the chair next to her desk. "No, I don't believe I should do that. I wouldn't want to create unfair competition for Bobby. I'd much rather he won the prize than I."

"A noble sacrifice," she teased, not quite able to repress a smile. "Did you want something?"

"Only your laughter, which I failed to obtain."

"I'll try harder next time. But now that you're here, I do have a question for you. I've been concerned about the burglaries we've had on the island lately."

"I believe we all are."

"It appears that the thief is targeting early Native American artifacts. I know the museum's collection is insured, but I wonder if we shouldn't take some additional safety measures and even request a new appraisal for insurance purposes."

"Interesting." Thoughtfully, he smoothed his fingertips over his mustache. "I knew, of course, that Wilma had lost a cedar mask. But I didn't realize other such artifacts had been stolen as well."

"Every household that's been victimized lost something of that nature, all of the pieces quite unique and valuable."

"In that case, thank you for sounding the warning. I'll give our insurance agent a call and alert him. And we'll all have to take extra care to be sure the alarm system's activated when we lock up the building at night."

Abby agreed that was an excellent precaution to take. But she suspected their salvation would be that Tucker Billings had not written the insurance policy for the conservatory. The thief wouldn't know the specific value of what was in their collection.

Hugo excused himself to take care of conservatory business. Abby finished up what she'd been doing, then headed out to talk with Jade Kebby.

AS SHE DROVE THROUGH TOWN, it seemed as though there was more traffic than there had been recently and more tourists strolling along the sidewalks. That was a sure sign of weekend visitors and a good omen for local businesses.

Parking in front of Billings' office, she walked up to the porch and opened the door. Jade was at her desk and looked up.

"Oh, hi, Dr. Stanton. Mr. Billings isn't in. Was he expecting you?"

"Actually, I came by to talk with you."

Looking surprised, the girl swiveled her chair around, away from her computer terminal. "I can get you some forms to fill out if you're wanting Mr. Billings to price out insurance coverage for you."

"No, that's not why I'm here." Abby took the guest chair next to Jade's desk. "I'd like to ask you some questions about the recent break-ins on the island."

"Well, sure, but the most I know is that the robberies have made a whole lot more work for me, processing all these claims. You know what I mean? Now I've gotta go through all the files to check the clients' coverage. You know, that's a really big job."

"I imagine that's true. I wonder, has anyone been here in the office besides you and Mr. Billings who had access to the files in the past couple of months?"

The girl's gaze slid toward the filing cabinet behind her, which was unlocked at the moment. "I don't think so."

"Not even accidentally? Someone could have been here in the reception area when you stepped away from your desk."

She shook her head. "Mr. Billings makes me be really careful about that."

"Sergeant Cobb and I suspect the thief is a young man. When we spoke with Mr. Billings, he thought you'd be more likely to know the younger generation of men in town than he does."

A blush colored her cheeks. "I know a few guys," she admitted, quickly adding, "but they aren't thieves."

"Maybe you've heard talk around town. Someone who's been bragging about having a lot of extra money all of a sudden. Maybe they bought a new truck? Something along those lines?"

She shook her head. "I haven't heard anything like that. But some of the guys I know don't live in Green Harbor. You know, they, like, come over from Friday Harbor, hang out or work, then go back on the ferry."

"I see. Then maybe you know Michael Romo or Darren Barber?"

"Why do you want to know about them?" The girl's dark brows had lowered into a frown.

"Oh, they're a couple of young men who've been working here for the past month or so. I thought maybe their paths might have crossed yours. You might move in the same crowd, you know."

Jade hesitated then said, "Darren talked me into going to dinner with him at the Springhouse Café one night." Fidgeting, she picked up a ballpoint pen on her desk, slid it into the top drawer, then straightened out some papers that didn't need straightening. "That's the only time I went out with him. Besides stinking of cigarette smoke, he's a real loser."

"That's too bad," Abby said while thinking that a young man with a criminal record might not be the best choice for a young woman to date. "What about Michael? Have you dated him too?"

The girl shrugged. "I don't really know him that well."

Abby didn't think she was making much progress and thought she'd try another tack. "Have any of your friends expressed any particular interest in Native American history or their antiquities?"

Jade's blush returned. "I'm part Indian, like an eighth or something. It's no big deal. But there's this one guy. He's really into that stuff. Kind of angry about it too."

"Angry? In what way?"

"Well, he claims the white man stole all the land from the Indians and then ruined it. You know, cut down the trees. Killed off all the salmon. And the government's out to destroy all the ancient peoples. Crazy stuff like that."

"I see. Did you date him?"

"Yeah, a couple of times." She shrugged. "But he was a real jerk. You know, he claimed I wasn't loyal enough to my ancestors. Shoot, I've got more Scottish and Hungarian ancestors than Lummi ones. That doesn't mean I have to go around wearing plaid and cooking goulash."

"No, I'm sure it doesn't." Abby almost smiled at the image. "Did he ever visit you here at the office?"

"Maybe once or twice. I don't remember."

The way Jade glanced away, Abby suspected the girl knew and didn't want to tell her. "What's this young man's name?"

"I don't want to get him in trouble. I mean, so he didn't like me. I wasn't Indian enough. It's no big deal."

Abby nodded. And waited.

Jade exhaled dramatically. "Oh, all right! It's Robb Phair. He works for the telephone company. He comes to Green Harbor maybe two or three times a week. But I haven't seen him in more than a month. Honest."

Her memory triggered, Abby recalled the uniform for telephone company employees was a dark shirt and pants. Mollie Berman, the school bus driver, had seen a telephone company truck in Opal Collins' neighborhood the Tuesday before that robbery. Abby further wondered if a telephone company employee would have access to or know how to clone a phone. Was she now seeing the puzzle pieces coming together? It certainly felt that way.

"Does Robb live in Friday Harbor?" she asked.

"Yeah. Way out of town in kind of a skuzzy cabin. His *ancestors* probably built it in the Stone Age. Like he's so proud of that."

It troubled Abby that Jade wasn't respectful of Native American culture, despite the fact she was some small part Lummi herself. That was a shame. The ancient cultures in the Northwest had a great deal to teach the rest of the world about living in harmony with nature and protecting the environment.

Abby came to her feet. "Thank you, Jade. You've been very helpful."

"People shouldn't go around stealing stuff, should they? Even if they're mad at the government."

"No, they shouldn't." But it might provide a strong motivation for a young man to strike back at those he felt had oppressed his people.

CHAPTER ❦ ELEVEN

AFTER TALKING WITH JADE, Abby drove directly to Henry Cobb's office. When she walked in, he was behind the counter talking with Deputy Artie Washburn. As she waited for the two men to finish their conversation, she noticed lines of fatigue etching Henry's face and a puffiness around his eyes. Last night's ordeal in front of the town council and local residents must have created a great deal of stress for him.

Finally, Artie nodded to a request Henry made of him and headed down the hallway toward the back of the station house.

Henry turned his attention to Abby. "Something I can do for you?" His voice sounded as weary as he looked.

"You must have had a hard night."

"Tell me about it. After I left the meeting, I learned there'd been a break-in and robbery on Lopez Island, so I headed over there. The resident got in late after a trip to the mainland and called it in about the time the council meeting started. I didn't get to bed until three o'clock. Back here by seven."

Abby was mentally rocked back on her heels. "What did they take this time?"

"Same MO. Cash, a laptop and a collection of hunting knives, including a couple of Indian knives with ivory handles."

Her heart skipped a beat. "Insurance?"

"Yep. His homeowner's policy is with an outfit that sells direct to current and former members of the military. Apparently that's a lot cheaper than any other insurance he could buy. He's retired Navy."

"Billings isn't his agent?" Her confidence that she'd found the connection between the crimes dissolved and disappointment shot through her. She'd been so sure Jade had given her the name of the thief.

Reading her mind, he said, "I'm disappointed too." He scrubbed his hand over his tanned face.

"Do you think it's the same thief? Or a copycat?"

"No way to be sure, but the break-in apparently happened late afternoon yesterday. He broke a window to gain entry, same as in the other robberies. No fingerprints. Had to be wearing gloves. Not much to go on."

"What about a phone call?"

"Nothing on the victim's voice mail. Phone company's checking their records now."

Idly, she picked up a flyer on the counter about the upcoming open mic night at Springhouse Café. At the moment, she didn't feel much like laughing.

"I just came from talking to Jade Kebby at Billings' office. She gave me a name. . . ." Her shoulders sank on a defeated sigh. "I was so sure I'd figured out who our thief is."

"Come on back to my office. At least I can get off my feet while you tell me what you found out."

If anything, Henry's in-basket was piled higher with Wanted notices and correspondence than it had been the last time Abby had visited his office. Like Jade, these break-ins had created more work for Henry than ever, and his resources were stretched thin. It didn't bode well that the robberies had spread to Lopez Island. Who knew where the next one would occur.

Henry sat down, tilted his chair back and tented his fingers under his chin. "So what did Jade have to say for herself?"

"She briefly dated a young man named Robb Phair, who lives on San Juan Island outside of Friday Harbor. Apparently he's an angry young man who works for the telephone company." She ticked off the reasons she'd thought Phair could be the guilty party, until she'd learned the Lopez robbery wasn't connected to Billings. "If Phair was getting his information from Jade, or looking through her files to find likely victims, how would he have known about the knife collection on Lopez?"

Henry lowered his chair and dragged a notepad across his desk. "I've been asking that question all night. We've missed something, but I'll be horse whipped if I can figure out what. This guy is good. Or maybe it's *guys* now."

"An accomplice?"

"Maybe." He jotted some notes on his pad of paper. "You get anything else out of Jade?"

"Only that she'd dated Darren Barber once and thought he was a loser. At the time, I thought it was possible Jade had passed on information about Billings' clients to Darren. I sensed she was holding back on me. But now I simply don't know what to think."

"Believe me, I'm part of that same club." He turned quiet as he wrote more notes on the yellow pad. "I'm going to run a background check on Jade, see if she's been in any trouble. And I'll run this new kid, Robb Phair, and ask the phone company people what they know about him."

"Particularly if he was assigned to Sparrow Island on the days of the break-ins," Abby suggested. "And now Lopez, I guess."

He nodded. "Depending on what I learn, maybe we can run a lineup for Mary. If we include Michael Romo—and I can find him—we've got three suspects."

"Mary isn't too confident she can identify the thief. She couldn't pick anyone out at last night's meeting."

"Maybe that's because our guy was still at Lopez doing his thing."

Abby conceded that was possible.

His phone rang. He picked it up, listened for a moment then returned the instrument to its cradle.

"The phone company traced a call made to the Lopez victim's house yesterday afternoon at about the time of the break-in. It's a cell phone that belongs to Naomi Yardley."

Abby's jaw dropped. "The librarian?"

"That's the only Naomi Yardley I know." He shoved his chair back from the desk. "Let's go have a talk with her."

BY MOST STANDARDS, the Sparrow Island Public Library was small. But Naomi Yardley, as head librarian, had seen to it that the book collection served the needs of the community. For children, she'd developed a research section that focused on the topics local teachers chose as subjects for student writing assignments.

While the fiction shelves were limited, there were plenty of titles to pique the interest of almost every youngster from pre-school through high school.

For both adult and juvenile requests, she tapped into a reciprocal system with both the county and the state. There were also three computers available to the public for Internet research.

The residents of Sparrow Island never felt deprived of access to the world of books and the information they provided.

As Abby walked into the library with Henry, she inhaled the combined scent of paper and bindings and glue that was unique to libraries. She remembered spending many hours here as a child, all of them deliciously fulfilling—including the one summer she'd consumed volumes of Nancy Drew.

They found Naomi changing the exhibits in the display case near the front door. She wore a skirt and blouse and low-heeled, sensible shoes.

"Good morning," Henry said, peering over the librarian's shoulder at the glass-topped display case. "What's your new exhibit about?"

Naomi, who was in her midforties, looked up and removed her glasses, letting them dangle from the chain hanging around her neck. She greeted them both with a smile. "We're coming up on the one-hundred-and-fiftieth anniversary of the start of the Pig War. I thought a few items from that era would be interesting. All of our fourth graders and eleventh graders are studying American history this quarter."

"The Pig War isn't exactly famous anywhere but in the islands," Abby said of the dispute that eventually settled the boundary between the San Juan Islands and Vancouver Island, which had been claimed by the British and was now a part of Canada.

"Ah, but it's the only war where loss of life was limited to one poor pig. That makes it a *good* war."

"Unless you're the pig," Abby countered with a smile. The display case contained maps of the area from the 1850s, military emblems, a canteen from the period and several photographs—almost everything contributed by the Sparrow Island Historical Society. To no one's surprise, Naomi was the longtime president of the group and devoted supporter.

"If you've got a minute, I'd like to talk to you," Henry said.

"Of course." Naomi closed the glass top of the display case and snapped the lock in place. "How can I help you?"

"Do you have a cell phone?" he asked.

About five feet two, she had to tip her head back to look up at Henry. "Yes. That is, I did. I lost my cell earlier this week and I haven't had a chance to buy a new one yet."

"Do you know where you lost it?"

"I'm not entirely sure. I spent the weekend with a friend in Friday Harbor. We saw a performance of *Macbeth* at the little theater there. I caught the ferry home Monday morning and came directly to work." She saw a library patron was ready to check out her books and walked over to the counter to help the woman.

Abby and Henry followed, waiting for her to conclude her business. While afternoons were generally busy at the library with lots of students doing their homework, mornings tended to be quiet. At the moment only one man was in the library, seated in a grouping of comfortable chairs and reading a copy of the *Seattle Times*.

"To tell you the truth," Naomi continued, picking up the conversation where she'd left off, "I didn't use my cell phone all weekend. I didn't even miss it until I was about to close up the library Monday evening and started to call a friend to meet me for dinner at the Springhouse Café."

"You didn't leave it at your friend's house?" Abby asked.

"I had her look for it. I thought maybe it had fallen under the bed. Or maybe it got stuck between the cushions of the couch in the living room. She's looked everywhere she could think of but couldn't find it. She called the little theater, too, thinking I might have dropped it there. Nothing." She shrugged. "I even called the ferry company and talked to lost and found. No one had turned my phone in."

"Did you try calling the number?" Henry asked.

"I did. But I remember turning the ringer off at the theater so if I got a call I wouldn't disrupt the performance. All I get is my own voice mail when I call myself."

"Which means, wherever the cell is, it isn't ringing," Abby concluded.

Pensive, Henry walked to the end of the counter and paced back. "Does your friend happen to have a son in his twenties who would have had access to your phone at the house?"

"She has a son, but he wasn't around much. He's not exactly into Shakespeare plays. He's more a monster-truck-with-big-wheels type." She frowned and tilted her head to one side. "Why do you ask?"

"Your cell phone has been implicated in a robbery on Lopez Island," Abby told her.

"*My* phone?" she gasped.

Henry declined to answer her question directly. "What's your friend's name and her son's?"

"Her name's Geri Spaulding, her son's Charles, but they call him Chuck. I'm sure he wouldn't be involved in anything illegal. He's never been great at academics, but he's a good kid."

Henry jotted down the names in his notepad. "Does Chuck have a job?"

"I think he works part-time for an auto repair place. He's very good with mechanical things, but it's been a bone of contention with Geri. She and her husband wanted Chuck to go to college."

"You say he likes those big monster trucks?" Henry continued.

"He bought one a few months ago. Tore it apart in their backyard, to Geri's consternation. But he's got it all back together now."

"Henry," Abby interrupted. "None of the witnesses recalled seeing a monster truck near the scene of the break-ins. They would have noticed, I'm sure."

"Just covering all the bases. Those trucks cost a lot of money for a kid who's only working part-time." He studied his notes a moment, then switched the subject. "Tell me who was on the ferry with you Monday morning."

"The other passengers?"

He nodded. "Any you can remember."

Looking baffled, she pulled up a stool and sat down behind the counter. "I'm not sure I paid any attention."

Abby realized Henry didn't want to lead Naomi by telling her exactly who they were looking for, but that would make it difficult for Naomi to recall who'd been onboard with her.

"Let's start with when you went onboard," Henry began. "You were in your car?"

She nodded.

"What other vehicles came onboard with you or parked near you?"

Concentrating, she stared off into the distance. Her hazel eyes narrowed. "I followed a white pickup truck down the ramp. It had one brake light out, which is why I remember that."

"Did the truck have any identification on it? A logo of some sort?"

Her focus returned to Henry. "It may have. I didn't notice. There were some construction supplies in the bed of the truck. Some long boards sticking out the back with a red bandana tied around the end of them."

Construction supplies might point to Darren Barber, Abby thought, but Naomi hadn't seen the driver of the truck clearly enough to identify him.

Henry led Naomi step-by-step through her arrival on the ferry, going up to the main deck, buying coffee and who she saw nearby during the hour-long journey.

"Most of the time I was reading a book," she admitted. "I suppose that's a librarian thing. I always have one with me. Guess I should learn to be more observant."

"It's a good habit to get into," Henry acknowledged. "Do you recall seeing any government workers, someone in a familiar uniform?"

"Oh! I saw that woman who's been harassing your father, Abby. About the donuts. She works for the state." Naomi chuckled. "What a dour person she is. She could use a little more sugar in her diet to sweeten her up."

"She does seem to be a bit over the top when it comes to eating healthy," Abby agreed. But to accuse Dorthea Gilmore of being the Sparrow Island thief was a real stretch. Beyond the fact that they were looking for a man, Abby had no reason to believe Dorthea had been on Lopez Island yesterday at the time of the break-in. She would have had to hurry to get back to Sparrow Island in time for last night's meeting.

"How 'bout someone from the telephone company?" Henry continued, getting more specific. "Or county road repair?"

"I simply don't know, Henry. I'm sorry. Maybe I saw a phone company truck, but I'm not even sure it got off at Green Harbor. It could've been going to some other island. Seems like they're always installing new lines or repairing something."

That certainly seemed to be the case, which meant Robb Phair could have access to all the islands. Including Lopez. But how would he have learned about the ivory-handled knives that were stolen?

Apparently running out of questions, Henry thanked Naomi for her time. He and Abby left the library and strolled back toward the sheriff's substation a block away.

"Do you think Naomi's friend's son is involved in this?"

"I think before we're done, half the twenty-year-old males in the county are going to be on my suspect list. Which means I've got nothing solid on any of them."

AFTER ABBY LEFT Henry and Naomi, she went to the Nature Museum to try to get some work done. But with little that was pressing on her desk, and feeling discouraged, Abby left her office midafternoon to drive home. She hadn't earned her keep as either an Associate Curator or as an amateur sleuth today, despite what she'd learned from Jade.

She hoped her subconscious would spend the weekend putting the confusing pieces of the puzzle together and come up with some answers by Monday.

Pulling into the driveway, she tapped the remote to open the garage door and drove inside. Maybe she should clear her head by going for a hike up toward Mount Ortiz. Fresh air and exercise would do her good.

She entered the house through the kitchen and found Mary sitting in the living room by the sliding glass door doing a crossword puzzle, Finnegan curled up on the floor nearby. An afternoon talk show played on the TV.

"You must be really bored, watching that program," Abby said.

"I managed to get out of the house this morning and go to the shop, but I wanted to be home again this afternoon in case—"

The phone in the kitchen rang.

"I'll get it." Abby did an about-face, crossed the kitchen and picked up the phone. "Hello."

For a moment, Abby heard nothing but silence, then the grinding sound of a diesel engine. That was followed by a click as the caller hung up, then the dial tone.

She stared at the phone. Slowly she became aware of the lumbering sound of an engine. Not on the phone. Outside the house. No more than a hundred feet away.

"Mary! Call Henry on your cell. That was the thief on the phone. He's somewhere nearby. I'm going to look for him." She dashed for the door into the garage.

"Wait for Henry!" Mary called after her.

"There isn't time."

The garage door seemed to take forever to lift. As soon as there was clearance, Abby backed her car out and onto the street. The school bus had already dropped off a few kids up the block and had pulled away.

Abby looked up and down the street. Other than the bus, there was only one vehicle in sight, a sedan turning the corner at the other end of the street. No telephone company truck. No pickup with construction supplies. Certainly not a monster truck with oversized tires.

Abby decided to follow the school bus. Maybe Mollie had seen something.

Speeding up the residential street, she caught up with Mollie at the next stop and pulled in front of the bus, blocking its way. She hopped out of her car and ran around to the other side of the bus. She climbed up the steps just as Mollie was about to close the door. There were only four students still seated.

"Hey, Abby, what's going on?" Mollie asked.

"Did you pass any trucks or cars in the last two blocks?" She was breathing hard, more from excitement than expended energy. She was so close to catching the thief.

Mollie blinked and frowned. "The UPS guy was a couple of blocks over."

"No, a truck of some sort just before you passed Mary's house."

"Mrs. Barthelow picked up Janie in their pickup," one of the girls in the back volunteered. "She has to go get a shot from the doctor."

"Probably in her butt," a boy added, snickering.

"Anything else?" Abby asked of both the children and Mollie. Of course, the youngsters didn't know why she was asking, which was just as well. Abby wouldn't have wanted to frighten them.

The kids shook their heads. Mollie did too.

"I'm sorry," Mollie said. "Between watching the road and keeping an eye on the kids so they don't kill each other, I didn't notice a thing."

Abby exhaled a discouraged breath. How could the thief have gotten away so quickly? "Well, keep an eye out anyway."

When she got back home, Mary was in the kitchen. She was wide eyed and the color had drained from her face.

"Did you catch him?"

"No. He had to have been right near the house. But by the time I got outside, he'd vanished." *The guy was a magician!* she thought.

Her eyes moist with tears, Mary's chin trembled. "He's still after Jacob's scrimshaw, isn't he?"

"I'm afraid so." In the process, he was also terrorizing Mary. That had to stop!

"I'm tempted to put the entire collection out in the front yard and let him have them all. I was so afraid if you caught up with him, he'd hurt you."

Realizing Mary's terror was not for herself, but for her safety as well, Abby knelt next to her sister and held her hands.

"We'll catch him, Mary. Soon." She prayed the Lord would help her keep that promise.

CHAPTER ✾ TWELVE

O N SATURDAY, WHEN ANTIQUE
dealer Richard Decker arrived from the mainland, he estimated the current worth of the scrimshaw collection at four
times the value of Mary's insurance coverage.

"If I weren't already sitting down," she said, "I think I'd
have fallen down. I had no idea the pieces had gone up in value
so much."

Standing with his hands behind his back, Richard continued to admire the collection in the cabinet. His navy blue
blazer, worn over a lighter blue mock turtleneck sweater, and
his dark hair graying at the temples made him look like a sea
captain—or the president of an exclusive yacht club, which he
was.

"Jacob made a good investment when he bought those
pieces," Abby commented. She'd been as shocked as Mary by
Richard's evaluation of the collection.

"He did make some astute decisions regarding his purchases." After one last admiring study of the collection, he sat down on the couch and leaned back. "The greatest part of the growth, however, has occurred in the past five years, with values rising exponentially in all of the handcrafts. Part of it is because of wealthy people searching for the best return on their investment. The remainder has to do with a sense of pride in one's region. In the Deep South, the value of handcrafted furniture and wood carvings from the eighteenth century have risen dramatically, and that's generally true in the Northeast as well."

"Here in the West, it's Native American antiquities that have benefitted from the increased interest," Abby concluded.

"That's correct." From his briefcase, he withdrew a property appraisal form and filled in the information about the collection and its worth.

When he'd finished, Mary wheeled closer to the couch. She took the form and studied it. "I'll have to notify my insurance agent immediately. The increased insurance will cost me a pretty penny, I imagine."

"That's true, I'm afraid. Basically, your late husband's collection is now irreplaceable at any price."

Abby took the overstuffed chair across from Richard. "If these handcrafted items bring such a high price these days, has there been an increase in thefts or black market activity?"

"Absolutely. There's been a ring of thieves working in Arizona and New Mexico stealing private collections of Navaho and Ute blankets and silver jewelry, then selling them through unscrupulous dealers to those who don't care about the items' provenance. In some cases, the dealers go so far as to forge ownership papers. Of course, there's a fair size market in counterfeit Native American crafts as well."

"So if someone stole Mary's scrimshaw collection, or say an ancient ceremonial mask, they couldn't simply take what they've stolen to the nearest pawn shop and get anything like what the pieces are worth."

"A pawnbroker wouldn't have any idea of the value of these items," Richard said. "A thief would be very foolish indeed if he simply tried to pawn them."

"Very interesting." Abby stood. "Would you like some tea or coffee, Richard? I think Mary has a supply of homemade cookies on hand, if you're interested."

His smile broadened, and he glanced toward Mary. "Now that's something I remember from my prior visits to your home. I must say, I envied your husband having a wife who was such a wonderful cook. I'm afraid my dearly beloved prefers to eat out. Although she does have other fine qualities, I hasten to add."

Mary blushed and laughed.

"Coffee, if you please," he said to Abby.

In the kitchen, Abby put on the coffee and got out a plate for a selection of oatmeal-raisin cookies and snickerdoodles that she found in the cookie jar.

As she got the coffee cups from the cupboard, she wondered how a young man would know how and where to find an outlet for whatever he stole—one of those unscrupulous dealers Richard spoke of. You'd hardly find them in the yellow pages. Maybe on the Internet? Or eBay?

Perhaps there was another way to track down the Sparrow Island thief.

When the coffee was ready, she carried a tray into the living room and set it down on the coffee table in front of the couch.

"Cream and sugar?" she asked as she poured a cup for Richard.

"Black is fine. That way I can save the calories for an extra cookie."

She smiled as she served him, then filled cups for herself and Mary. After she'd passed around the plate of cookies, she settled down in the overstuffed chair again.

"Richard, would you know any of those 'unscrupulous' dealers you mentioned who specialize in Native American antiquities, particularly here in the Northwest?"

He used a napkin to wipe the corners of his mouth. "Mary just told me about the attempted robbery you've experienced and what's been happening in the area. Terrible."

"I think it's possible a dealer may be working with the thief," Abby said. "Otherwise, whoever's stealing all these artifacts wouldn't know how to turn them into cash."

"You're quite right, of course. As it happens, I haven't heard any rumors of late. In fact, this is the first that I've heard of your rash of robberies."

Apparently William's stories in the *Birdcall* weren't being picked up by mainland media.

"I'll have to nose around, as they say," Richard continued. "It may take me a day or two to dig out the information you need."

"The sooner the better," Abby told him. She had the troubling feeling that when Mary increased her insurance coverage, the thief would hear the news and be all the more determined to get his hands on the scrimshaw collection.

They visited for a while longer, Richard bringing Mary up to date on his children and new grandchildren.

Finally, he stood. "If I'm going to get home for dinner, I'll need to catch the next ferry."

Mary extended her hand to him. "Thank you so much for coming, Richard. You were always a good friend to Jacob, and I appreciate your help too."

"You're more than welcome." Turning to Abby, he shook her hand too. "I'll get back to you about dealers with a questionable reputation. I hope the authorities can stop this thief soon. It's bad for us all."

Abby and Mary escorted him out the front door. As they waited on the porch while Richard got into his car, a Labrador retriever with a smooth, dark coat came bounding across the street, his tail wagging. Less than a year old, he hadn't yet grown into his big feet or floppy ears. He came to a halt on the walkway.

"Hello, boy, where'd you come from?" Mary said.

The dog darted toward Finnegan, then hopped away as though asking a new friend to come out and play. Finnegan ignored the invitation.

Richard waved from his car, then drove off. Mary and Abby waved in return.

"I haven't seen this puppy around before." Abby held out her hand for the dog to sniff her.

"I wish people would better train their dogs to stay on their property. It's so easy for them to be struck by a car or run off and get lost."

Kneeling, Abby stroked the dog's neck. "He doesn't have a collar."

"Maybe he's already lost."

Just then they heard a penetrating whistle. The dog alerted, then whirled and raced off down the street in the same galloping stride that had brought him into Mary's yard.

"Apparently he lives nearby."

"Well, I for one, hope the owner trains him better to stay at home."

Abby agreed. Not only were dogs running loose a danger to themselves, they posed a problem for ground nesting birds in the neighborhood.

SUNDAY MORNING, after the choir sang a spirited version of "Joyful, Joyful, We Adore Thee," Rev. James Hale took his place behind the handmade altar made of madrone wood. A slender man with blond hair who wore wire-rimmed glasses, he appeared younger than his forty-five years.

He looked toward the choir and smiled. "That was indeed joyful and it puts our hearts in exactly the right mood for this morning's topic. Thank you."

Mary sat at her regular place at the end of the shortened pew. Henry, who was coming to dinner at Stanton Farm after the service, was next to her. Abby and her parents sat beyond him.

She smiled when she noted the morning's program indicated Rev. Hale's sermon was entitled "Laughter is a Gift from God." She wondered if his sermon would include a bit of stand-up comedy, perhaps a rehearsal for his performance at the Springhouse Café.

The pastor turned back to the audience. "I'm sure many of you have heard that the Springhouse Café will soon be hosting

an open mic night for stand-up comics. That got me to thinking about laughter and what it means in our lives. I know one
of the most glorious sounds I've ever heard is the sound of my
son Toby giggling. What a blessing for any parent."

A good many heads around Mary nodded in agreement.
Two-year-old Toby was a darling boy, full of life and good spirits.
He would bring joy to anyone's heart. All of those who were
parents were no doubt remembering their own children's
laughter bringing them joy too. Zack and Nancy had certainly
done that for Mary.

"So I did what I always do when I'm preparing my sermon,"
Rev. Hale continued. "I turned to the Bible to see what the
Word of God has to say about laughter.

"In Proverbs 31, Solomon describes the virtues of the wife
of noble character and compares her strength and dignity to
her ability to laugh at the days to come. Some days, that must
be very difficult for a wife. We husbands have been known to
make life hard for our wives." He glanced in the direction of
his wife, Patricia, and winked. "A man is doubly blessed by a
wife who can laugh at his foibles."

A chuckle rippled around the audience. Everyone knew
James and his wife were a loving couple. Mary imagined there
was lots of laughter in their home.

"There, you see?" Rev. Hale said. "We laugh together and
that brings us all joy.

"Laughter comes at those moments when we have something to celebrate. David recorded such a moment in
Psalm 126:1–3. 'When the Lord brought back the captives to
Zion, we were like men who dreamed. Our mouths were filled
with laughter, our tongues with songs of joy. Then it was said

among the nations . . . The Lord has done great things for us, and we are filled with joy.'"

The pastor went on to reference other moments of laughter in the Bible, and Mary recalled those times in her life with family and friends when they had all laughed together. Just remembering the good times lifted her spirits and helped to press away her worry about the thief who seemed determined to steal Jacob's scrimshaw collection.

"So now we know laughter is God's gift to us," he continued. "In fact, modern science agrees. Laughter's good for us. When we laugh, we breathe deeply. Our circulation improves. Laughing reduces stress. It's aerobic. It's even been said laughter is healthier than eating chocolate!"

Everyone laughed at that.

Holding out his arms to the congregation palms up, he said, "I want you all to stand now. We're going to laugh together. Little giggles and great belly laughs. Together!"

Somewhat hesitantly, the congregation rose.

In a good imitation of Santa Claus, he lowered his voice. "Ho ho ho." He urged the group on. "Let me hear you laugh! Ha ha ha!"

Mary found herself laughing. Not loud at first. But as she looked around, she discovered it was contagious. She couldn't help herself. Apparently no one else could either. The laughter rolled and echoed around the chapel and sun streamed in through the circular stained-glass window at the back of the sanctuary. If a stranger had walked into the church at that moment, he would have thought they had all gone mad.

Finnegan looked up from his place at Mary's feet as though he had already come to that conclusion.

Mary could not remember when she'd had that much fun at church, accepting the Lord's gift.

The congregation continued to laugh and be in high spirits as they filed out of the church.

Bobby came running up to Mary. "Wasn't that great!" He did a happy jig that would have done his Scottish ancestors proud. "That's what's gonna happen at our open mic night. Everybody's gonna be laughing like crazy!"

Mary tugged him closer for a hug. "At your jokes, not mine."

"Sure they will. Your jokes are great." The boy looked up at Henry, who was pushing her wheelchair. "Are you gonna enter the contest, Sergeant?"

Henry nearly choked. "Not me, Bobby. I don't tell jokes."

"I could help you write some. You know, like how weird it is to be a cop. Stuff like that."

Mary smothered a laugh with her hand.

"Uh, Bobby, being a cop isn't weird. It's important. And it's hard work." Although Henry wasn't dressed in his uniform this morning, he still looked sharp in a sport coat and slacks. Over the years, he'd kept himself in good shape and his physique showed it.

"Well, sure, being a deputy sheriff is hard. We all know that." The youngster rolled his eyes up as though he was think-ing. When he spoke, he lowered his voice to imitate Henry's. "It's hard being a policeman. Every time I meet someone new, they're afraid I'm going to arrest them. I don't know why they think that." Bobby did a twirling motion with his hand. "Maybe it has something to do with these handcuffs I carry around."

Henry laughed and Mary nearly doubled over.

When she recovered her breath, she said, "I think Bobby could work up a winning routine for you, Henry, if you'd like to enter the contest. The prize is a free Sunday brunch for four."

"Not me," he insisted, still sputtering. "I'm happy to buy my own brunches. But he may have a future as a writer for Comedy Central."

Bobby beamed. "I've been thinking about that. But I want to be an astronaut first."

Hooking his arm around the boy's shoulders and grinning, Henry said, "I can see it now. The first sitcom from outer space. An overnight hit."

AS ELLEN, ALONG WITH MARY and Abby, went to work in her kitchen to prepare their Sunday supper, she said, "Rev. Hale's sermon was very timely. Several of the volunteers at the Visitor Center are planning to perform at the open mic night. Or their husbands are."

"It ought to be a fun evening." Using pot holders, Abby lifted a casserole dish out of the oven and placed it on the stove top.

"We'd better get there early," Mary said. "I don't want to miss Bobby's performance."

Working as a team, the three of them got everything on the table and called the men to supper. Conversation during the meal was light and filled with the joy of friendship and love.

After everyone had enjoyed their servings of roasted chicken, cornbread stuffing and a delicious green bean casserole, Abby and her mother cleared the dining room table. For dessert, they served bread pudding with pecans and flavored with maple syrup.

Henry groaned with pleasure. "Mrs. Stanton, you're trying to spoil me again."

"It's her way of counteracting that Gilmore woman and her war against cholesterol." George chuckled. "But you watch, we'll win the battle in the end. We have a new plan."

"Now, George," Ellen said, "you know we don't eat like this every day. Only on Sundays. Besides, I used a low calorie-syrup."

"All the more reason that it's fine to have a donut now and again," George insisted.

"What's your new plan, Dad?" Abby spooned a bite of bread pudding into her mouth and savored the sweet taste. Her mother and Mary were by far the best cooks in the family, while her own efforts rarely extended beyond the simplest meals.

"We're starting a letter-writing campaign. The governor's going to hear from us and so is every other elected official we can think of."

"At least a letter-writing campaign won't block traffic, Mr. Stanton," Henry said. "I'd hate to have to arrest Mary's father for obstructing a public thruway."

"We'll try to avoid that," he responded.

"I pity Dorthea Gilmore," Mary said. "I'm sure she thinks she's doing the right thing, trying to protect the health of the men in your club. She had no idea how territorial you all are about your donuts."

"I think she's beginning to catch on." George gave Mary a sly grin and continued to consume his bread pudding with gusto.

Finally, when everyone had finished their dessert, Abby decided to broach the topic that had been on their minds for the past couple of weeks.

"Henry, did Mary tell you about the new appraisal she got on her scrimshaw collection?"

"I haven't had time," she admitted. "But I have been thinking I'd better get home soon. I don't like to leave the house empty for too long at a time."

Henry patted her hand. "I think you're all right to stay awhile. I asked Artie to take a drive by your place every half hour or so while he's on patrol today. And the fact is, the thief hasn't hit any homes over the weekends so far. That leads me to believe he doesn't live here and probably only works here during the week. Working here's his cover if he gets caught in a neighborhood."

"Thank you, Henry. That eases my mind some."

"Now tell me about this appraisal you had done."

Mary recounted their visit with Richard Decker and what he'd said. When she mentioned the new value he'd placed on the collection, George Stanton whistled.

"No wonder you're worried about having the collection stolen," he said.

"I'm planning to call Tucker Billings to increase my insurance coverage. Not that money could ever replace the sentimental value of the collection."

Both George and Ellen acknowledged that would be the case.

"I asked Richard how the thief would fence . . . I guess that's the correct term," Abby said, "fence all of the artifacts that have been stolen. Richard didn't think the thief would get much value from an ordinary pawnbroker."

"Probably not," Henry agreed. "I've notified pawnshops in the state to be on the lookout for the stolen items, but we haven't had any reports back yet. The stolen laptops and silver pieces might eventually show up. I wouldn't think a cedar ceremonial mask would, though. Of course, the stolen cash is impossible to trace."

Abby agreed that was probably true.

"Tucker brought his client list of those insured for valuable artifacts around to the office yesterday," Henry said. "Twenty-nine households, including those who've already been robbed. I contacted all but two, suggesting they take extra precautions."

"I do hope Tucker isn't involved in this scheme," Ellen said. "We've known him since he was just a little boy and have been friends with his father. It'd be such a shame if he were guilty of something."

"I don't make him for the thief," Henry said. "But he's involved in some way, although his role may be unintentional. The thief's getting his information from a good source and he knows how to dispose of the merchandise for the biggest profit."

"Richard's going to ask around—see if he can get a lead on a dealer who might not care that the artifacts are stolen property," Abby said.

"That's good," Henry said. "Have him get back to me if he comes up with anything."

"I will."

"I just wish I could put some sort of an invisible force field around the display to protect it," Mary mused.

"You know, maybe we can do that," Henry said. "Before you call Billings, call Aaron Holloway. He's good with computers and electronics. I bet he could wire the cabinet to set off an alarm if someone breaks into it. Our thief wouldn't get far with a lot of bells and whistles going off.

"Meanwhile, I'm going to bring in our three suspects tomorrow for questioning. I'd like you to come down to the station house to see if you can ID anyone."

"All right." Mary started to stack the dirty dishes to take them into the kitchen. "But I can't promise I'll recognize the man."

CHAPTER ❦ THIRTEEN

Monday afternoon Abby met Mary at the sheriff's substation for the lineup Henry had arranged. She wanted to take another look at the two workmen she'd identified as possible suspects and see if Robb Phair fit Mary's description.

"Did Aaron have a chance to get over to the house?" Abby asked her sister as they waited in the reception area of the station.

"He did. When he finished hooking up all the wires, he tested the alarm. It was so loud, it practically scared the spokes right out of my wheelchair."

Picturing the metal spokes suddenly flying all around the living room, Abby laughed out loud.

"Well, maybe it wasn't quite that bad," Mary admitted with a grin. "But it did send Blossom racing under my bed. And poor Finnegan whined and tried to cover his ears with his paws." She gave the dog an affectionate scratch in his ruff. "Even so, he stayed right beside me."

"Sounds like the alarm would scare off a burglar."

"And give anyone in the house a heart attack if they weren't expecting it."

"I hope Aaron showed you how to turn it off so you can get into the cabinet without the alarm sounding."

Mary nodded that he had just as Henry appeared from the back of the station house.

"Sorry to keep you waiting, ladies."

He gestured for them to come with him, and they did, Abby pushing Mary's chair. They stopped in front of a one-way window that revealed four men standing with their backs to them. Each had dark hair and was wearing a dark jacket and pants and work boots of one type or another. They each wore a ball cap.

"They can't see or hear us," Henry said. "So don't worry about that, Mary. I want you to take a close look and tell me if any of these men look like the one you saw running away from your house after the break-in. Take your time. I want you to be sure."

"I thought you only had three suspects," Mary said.

"One or more of those men may not be suspects at all."

"You're trying to trick me?" she asked.

"No, I want to be sure if you make a positive identification that we've got the right guy."

While Mary studied the men, Abby did too. They were all about the same build, about five feet nine or ten, around a hundred and seventy pounds. From the tattoo on his neck, she recognized number one as Darren Barber, the man who was working on the repair of the docks and had a police record. It looked as though he'd had a recent haircut.

Number three had the loose-limbed stance of Michael

Romo, who had fled the road resurfacing crew when she asked to talk to him.

Number four looked familiar somehow, but she couldn't recognize him from the back. That left number two, who she guessed was Robb Phair. He stood ramrod straight, the rigid set of his shoulders suggesting he was not happy being in a lineup. She wondered if that was because he was guilty, or simply an angry young man.

"I'm just not sure," Mary finally said.

Henry's expression didn't change. "That's all right, Mary. Only identify the man if you're sure."

"I think it could be either number two or four."

"Does that mean you're sure it's not number one and three?" he asked.

"Well, I don't remember seeing a tattoo on the man's neck. But I suppose it could have been covered up by his jacket."

"What about number three?"

"He looks too skinny to me. It seems to me the robber was thicker across the back." With her fingertips, she rubbed her temple. "I'm sorry, Henry. I wish I could be more confident, but I simply can't tell for sure."

"It's okay. You tried." He gave her shoulder a reassuring pat, then pressed the button on an intercom. "Let numbers one and three go, and put number two in the interrogation room." He pulled down a shade so they could no longer see the suspects.

"What about number four?" Abby asked.

"He's a new recruit in the sheriff's department. I asked him to come over from Friday Harbor because he fit Mary's description. He grew up here on Sparrow Island."

Mary gasped. "Oh, for pity's sake! Did I identify a sheriff's deputy?"

His lips tilting into a half smile, Henry said, "I think he has a solid alibi for the day in question, so I'll let him go this time."

At a sound behind them in the hallway, they all turned to see Deputy Mike Bennett escorting the number two suspect into the interrogation room as the others were released.

Suddenly, Finnegan was on his feet and braced, his head lowered and facing toward the closed door. Low in his throat, he released a threatening growl.

"Finnegan, hush!" Mary gripped his harness. "Sit."

Abby made eye contact with Henry.

"Interesting," he commented, his focus on the doorway the two men had passed.

"Do you think Finnegan recognized that man as the one who broke into Mary's house?" Abby asked.

Scratching his fringe of graying hair, Henry said, "Not in a way that would stand up in court, but it certainly suggests I ought to ask that young man some hard questions."

The hope they were finally getting somewhere sparked in Abby's chest. "I'd like to sit in on the questioning, if that's all right."

"I would too," Mary said. "To think that young man—"

"Not you, Mary. You're a witness," Henry said.

"Why don't you go on home, Mary?" Abby suggested. "I'll let you know what happens later."

IF IT WEREN'T for the rigid set of his jaw, the downturn of his mouth and his angry dark eyes, Abby thought Robb Phair would have been a handsome young man. His black hair, straight nose and prominent cheek bones proclaimed his proud Native American ancestry.

Henry sat across a small table from Robb; Abby sat next to the sergeant.

"What's this all about?" Robb demanded, his fists planted firmly on the table. "How come you let those other guys go?"

"One of the witnesses ID'd you, Phair."

Only the canine witness, Abby thought, keeping her expression neutral. It was legal for the police to mislead a suspect, even lie to them.

Robb shot a seething look at Abby. "You're crazy. You dragged me off the ferry and messed up my work schedule because of her? She ID'd me for what? I've never seen this broad in my life."

"The witness saw you when you broke into her house. You jackrabbitted out of there like the coward you are."

"You got nothin' on me." He leaned back in his chair and folded his arms across his chest, but didn't relax his fists.

"We've had you on our radar for a couple of weeks now. Jade Kebby fingered you, and now we've got our witness."

The young man's eyes widened momentarily. "Jade? What's she got to do with this?"

"Why don't you tell me," Henry said. "Was she your accomplice? Maybe your getaway driver? Or did she just tell you which houses to rob?"

He tried to stare down Henry, but Abby knew that wasn't going to work. Neither would the young man's implied threat of using his fists.

"Jade tells me you think that white men stole the land from Native Americans," Abby said. "Is robbing people your way of getting revenge?"

He remained stoically silent.

"Did you know one of the people you stole from is a Native American and a leader in the Salish tribe?"

He jutted out his jaw. "I wouldn't steal from my own people."

"Maybe Jade didn't tell you. Maybe she didn't care," Henry said. "She's not as proud of her ancestry as you are. Maybe she's just plain greedy."

Robb's eyes darted between Henry and Abby. "I don't know what you're talking about. I want a lawyer."

"You're not under arrest, Phair. Right now you're only what we call a person of interest. If you lawyer up, I'll have to arrest you. I don't think you want that."

"Tell us about you and Jade," Abby urged.

"There's nothing to tell. I dumped her. So she's mad at me and trying to hang something on me that I didn't do. She's lying through her teeth. She didn't tell me nothin' about robbing anybody." He glared at Henry. "Either arrest me or let me go. I don't care which. Either way, I don't have nothin' more to say." He clamped his mouth shut.

Henry seemed to contemplate his next move. Abby suspected without an ID made by a human rather than a dog, he didn't have enough evidence to make an arrest. But he was clearly reluctant to let the young man go.

"I'm going to let you go. For *now*," he emphasized. "But I want you to think about what we've said here. Somebody's setting you up. It'll go a lot easier on you if you come clean with me sooner rather than later. You got that?"

Robb shoved his chair back so hard when he got up that it fell over backwards with a crash. "Yeah, I got it." He stalked out of the interrogation room.

Abby blew out a long breath. "We didn't exactly get a confession, did we?"

"Not even close." Leaning his elbows on the table, Henry rested his head in his hands. "I'm going to have to put a fire under the telephone company to get Phair's records. If the dates and times match up, we'll know he's our guy. Then we'll dangle some bait in front of his nose."

"What about the other two suspects? Do you think they're in the clear?" With no evidence against them, she felt guilty for having suspected them of the crimes in the first place. She'd definitely been jumping at shadows.

"I won't rule them out entirely, but I sure can't make a case against them. If one or the other is guilty, they'll be tempted by the same bait we dangle for Phair."

THE NEXT MORNING, the weather had turned cloudy again. A fine mist forced Abby to turn on the windshield wipers as she drove to work.

The parking lot was nearly empty, the asphalt blackened by the rain. Not much chance of a big crowd of visitors on such a rainy day.

Her first stop was at the terrarium pupae display.

Wilma walked up behind her. "I think those things are dead."

"Entirely possible. I had thought they'd emerge by now." Tilting her head and adjusting her glasses, Abby studied the pupa on the cabbage leaf. "Maybe rain and cold weather slows down the process. I've only seen one moth this spring in my neighborhood." And Blossom had done her best to catch the poor thing.

"Abby, how would those little creatures know that it's raining outside? They've been in here where it's warm for more than a week."

She glanced at her friend. "Good question." Offhand, she couldn't think of an entomologist she could call. Maybe, if she had time, she should do an Internet search.

Or, for a change, she could try to be patient.

RIGHT AFTER LUNCH, Mary received a call on her cell phone from Henry.

"The phone company came through," he said. "Robb Phair was assigned to repair work on Sparrow Island every day that we had a robbery."

"Then he's the thief?" How sad such an angry young man had decided to break the law out of misguided loyalty to his ancestry.

"It's sure looking like it. The only glitch I see is that he wasn't on Lopez the day of that robbery, at least as far as I can tell."

She glanced toward the kitchen door as though the thief might be standing outside ready to break in. "What do we do now?"

"I want you to go over to Billings' office. Take the new appraisal with you and ask to have your insurance increased."

Automatically, Mary nodded. "I can do that this afternoon."

"Be sure Jade knows why you're there and how much you're increasing your insurance."

"So you do think she's involved?"

"My gut feeling's pretty strong. Again, without proof I can't make an arrest and I don't want to tip her off yet. Though, if she is involved, Phair may have already told her we're on to them."

"In which case, our trap won't work."

"It'll work. That scrimshaw collection is too valuable for

them to pass up. Which is why I want both you and Abby out of the house tomorrow afternoon. I've arranged with the phone company to have Phair assigned here tomorrow."

Her heartbeat picked up. "You expect them to act that fast?"

"I think they'll hit your house one more time, figuring they're making a big killing, and then try to make their getaway to the mainland to cash in on the last of the loot they've taken."

"But if I'm not here to call—"

"Artie Washburn will be there. He's got a vested interest in getting his aunt's ceremonial mask back and nailing the guy. He'll catch the thief in the act, make the arrest, and we'll be able to wrap this all up by dinnertime tomorrow."

Mary sincerely hoped that would be the case.

After she hung up, Mary got her coat and rain hat from the closet, and tucked Richard's signed document safely in her purse where it would stay dry.

"Come on, Finnegan. We have to go bait a trap." He seemed as eager as she to catch the thief, although Mary ventured he wasn't nearly as nervous.

The rain was falling fairly hard by the time she got to Billings' office, which made the trip from the van to the front door uncomfortable. Water dripped off her hat as Finnegan helped pull her up the ramp to the door. She pushed it open and worked her way inside.

"Oh, gosh, can I help you?" Jade scurried out from behind her desk, her sandals clapping on the carpet.

"I think I've got it, thanks." Taking off her hat, she gave it a shake. Finnegan did the same with his body. "I'm Mary Reynolds, one of Tucker's clients."

"Yes, ma'am, I know who you are."

It often amazed Mary how many people in town knew her even when she hadn't actually met them. Surely that came from living in a small town all of her life.

"I've brought Tucker a new estimate of value on my scrimshaw collection. With all the robberies that've been happening in town, I was afraid the collection had appreciated so much that I didn't have enough coverage." She retrieved Richard's official papers from her purse. "You can imagine how shocked I was when I discovered I was underinsured by several thousand dollars." The girl's eyes widened when Mary handed her the paperwork and she read the new value.

"Wow! Mr. Billings will want to know about this right away."

So will the thief, Mary thought.

Tucker must have heard them talking. He stepped out of his office to see who had arrived.

"Mary!" He crossed the reception area and took her hand. "I didn't know you were dropping by this afternoon. What can I do for you?"

She repeated her need for increased insurance. Asking Jade to make a copy of the new estimate, Tucker took Mary into his office.

A half hour later, when she returned to her van, Mary felt as though she'd placed a very tempting morsel of cheese in a rat trap. Now all they had to do was wait to see who took the bait.

Pulling away from the curb, she noticed a sedan with a woman driver taking the empty space she'd left. Probably another of Tucker's clients. His business seemed to be thriving.

On the way home, she stopped at the Green Grocer to pick up some wild salmon that was on sale, whole wheat rolls and fresh greens for dinner. School had just let out and youngsters were crowding around the checkout counter to buy their snacks.

A few minutes later, as she rolled into her kitchen, the grocery bag in her lap, the phone rang. Without thinking, she picked up the phone. "Hello."

Her greeting was met with silence.

Fear arced through her. "Who's there?"

Click. The dial tone hummed in her ear. Her hand shook. Air lodged painfully in her lungs. *How could the thief know about the insurance increase so soon?*

The answer was more than apparent. Either Jade or Tucker Billings hadn't wasted any time letting him know.

CHAPTER ❦ FOURTEEN

Glorify the Lord with me; let us exalt his name together.
I sought the Lord, and he answered me;
he delivered me from all my fears (Psalm 34:3–4).

THE SCRIPTURE for Abby's morning devotionals seemed particularly appropriate on a day when Henry hoped to catch a thief breaking into Mary's house. The words calmed Abby and gave her faith that all would go well and no one would be hurt. The phone call yesterday afternoon had terrified Mary more than any of the other calls.

Abby, too, for that matter.

Since it was still cool and gloomy outside, after getting dressed, she had carried her coffee into the living room and sat next to the sliding glass door while she read. Blossom cruised around her legs in a friendly morning greeting. Outside the window, the gray light of dawn struggled to bring color to the landscape and the pulsing ocean beyond.

The doorbell chimed, startling her.

Wondering who it could be at such an early hour, she set her book aside and went to the door. Through the peephole she saw William Jansen standing on the front porch.

"You're up and out early," she said when she opened the door. He looked none too happy about the early hour, which probably had something to do with the dozen copies of the *Birdcall* he had in his arms.

"I brought you your paper." Wearing a hat and raincoat, he thrust the plastic-wrapped newspaper toward her.

"Does this mean Lynell Cowan missed us again?" She could only believe Lynell must have developed a senility problem, though he hardly seemed old enough to be losing touch with reality.

"He delivered the paper just fine. I parked down the street where he couldn't see me and waited for him to come by. He tossed every paper right where he should." He smoothed his mustache with his fingertips, which did nothing to tame the bushy effect. "Then I decided to stick around for a while. Good thing I did too."

"What happened?" She peered around outside thinking she might get a clue why William was so upset.

"A dog happened, that's what."

Abby blinked. "A dog?"

"Yep. Some mutt from down the street came running out of his house and made a circuit of the neighborhood. He made many trips and took every paper that Lynell had delivered on the entire block, carried them back to his house and stuffed them under his porch."

"Oh my . . ." She was pretty sure the mutt in question was the young Labrador retriever who'd wandered into their yard and wanted to play with Finnegan. "Did you talk with the dog's owner?"

"You can bet I did. He denied everything until I showed him the pile of papers under his house. Then he claimed he'd been teaching the dog to bring in his own paper, not everybody else's."

"Clever dog." The dog had probably gotten so much praise from his owner for doing his job well, that he decided bringing home more papers would earn him even more tasty snacks.

William humphed. "Clever or not, I told the guy I was going to start charging him for ten subscriptions if his dog kept it up. That got his attention."

"I'm sure it did." Subscribing to the *Birdcall*, however, wasn't a big item for anyone's budget. "At least you found out the missing papers weren't Lynell's fault."

"Yeah, I did. And as soon as I get the rest of these papers delivered, I'm going to call him and apologize." He didn't seem happy about that, either.

"Well, I'm glad you solved the Mystery of the Missing Papers."

He grunted something unintelligible and walked away with his armload of newspapers.

Smiling to herself, Abby closed the door behind him and slipped the newspaper out of its plastic wrapper. Unfolding the paper, her gaze fell on yet another photo of the Men's Club protest over their precious donuts. She'd never realized how stubborn her father and his friends could be.

Below that was a short article about the upcoming open mic night at Springhouse Café. It seemed the number of would-be comics planning to participate was growing rapidly, including comics from other islands.

Abby hoped Bobby understood he'd have some stiff competition.

SHORTLY AFTER ONE O'CLOCK, Mary opened the door for Deputy Artie Washburn.

Removing his hat, he stepped inside. "Everything all right?" he asked.

"So far. But I'm worried about you here all alone."

"I'll be fine, Mary."

"But what if the thief has a gun?"

He gave her a grin that dimpled his cheek. "I've got one too."

"I'm being silly, aren't I?"

"Not silly at all. Aunt Wilma worries about me all the time. It's kinda nice, actually." He glanced up the stairs and then walked to the living room. "Back door locked?"

"Absolutely. Oh, I didn't bolt the front door." She wheeled around—

"I'll get it." He dropped his cap on the coffee table. "You and Finnegan can go now. I've got everything under control here."

Still troubled, she said, "How are you going to arrest the man all by yourself?"

"As soon as I hear the phone ring, I'll call for backup. Henry, or Deputy Bennett, will be here, probably before I get the cuffs on the guy. Meanwhile, I figure I've got pretty soft duty, just sitting around looking at the scenery."

She exhaled a worried sigh. "Will you have Henry or someone call me as soon as you arrest the man?"

"I'll see to it, Mary. I promise."

"There're cookies in the cookie jar, and you can make yourself a cup of coffee or tea if you'd like."

"Thanks. I may just do that." He stood waiting for her to leave, and finally she had no choice but to go.

She'd considered spending the afternoon with her parents, but decided against that, not wanting to worry them about the trap Henry had set. Instead, she went to Island Blooms to while away the time until she heard the news the thief was under arrest.

Inside the shop, she found Candace bobbing and weaving and dancing to music that featured a guitar, drums and an instrument that sounded like a cat being stepped on. She winced when the cat hit a particularly high note.

"Hi, Mary." Candace had to shout to be heard over the music. "I didn't know you were coming in this afternoon."

"I have to stay out of the house for a few hours." Mary sent a distressed look toward the boom box on the shelf in the back room.

"Oh, let me turn that off!" She danced across the room and switched the music off. "Sorry about that. There wasn't anyone here, so I thought I'd listen to something a little different."

"It sounded like a cat was being killed."

Candace laughed. "The leader of the group plays a Jinghu, a Chinese two-stringed fiddle. It's played in Chinese operas. Cool, huh?"

Mary didn't think it would catch on in the States.

"Why do you have to be out of the house?" Candace asked.

Mary told her about the trap they'd baited for the thief. "I thought, as long as I'm here, I'd keep busy by putting together a couple of wreaths out of our dried materials. We're down to just a few in stock, and they usually sell well once tourist season starts."

"Good idea. I'll give you a hand."

While Candace got the stored materials out of the cupboard, Mary released Finnegan from his harness so he could move around more freely. He gave himself a shake, then settled down nearby, ready to pick up anything she might drop.

Candace placed three boxes of neatly organized materials on the worktable. "Here we go."

To begin forming the wreath, Mary arranged dried wild grasses on a circular wicker-like frame using glue and thread, weaving them in. Most of the dried materials had been gathered on Sparrow Island. Some she had bought from Ana Dominguez. Other bits and pieces had been collected by Abby or Henry or some other friend while they were hiking through the wilder regions of the island.

Mary loved to contrast the golden shades of the grass and their feathery tips with darker seedpods, some almost as large as her fist. Dried berries and pressed wildflowers provided a touch of color.

While she worked, she kept glancing at the big clock on the wall. It ticked off the seconds with aching slowness. As time passed, her anxiety grew. Why hadn't the thief struck yet? Or had he already showed up, overwhelmed Artie and stolen every last piece of Jacob's collection? She couldn't get the image of the empty display case out of her mind.

Finally, she leaned back and watched Candace working on her wreath, her strawberry-blonde hair cascading past her shoulders. "That's very nice," Mary said.

Sitting across the worktable, Candace looked up and smiled. "Thank you. You're a nervous wreck, aren't you?"

"Does it show that much?"

"No, but I know I'd be going crazy if I thought someone was going to steal the Indian basket I bought last spring. It cost me way more than I should have spent, but I love it. The workmanship is exquisite."

"So is the scrimshaw we're using for bait. Beautifully hand carved."

"After hearing about all the break-ins, I've hidden my basket way in the back of my closet, inside my suitcase. I'm hoping if the thief shows up at my place, he'll have a hard time finding it."

"Oh my, I hope he has no idea you even own such a thing, much less be able to find it if he does."

"Yeah, me too."

For a few minutes, Mary tried to continue working on the wreath, but she had trouble concentrating.

"Has Brad come up with any more lawyer jokes for open mic night?" she asked Candace.

"Oh, yes. He seems to be on a roll now." Setting her scissors aside, she focused on a middistance beyond Mary's shoulder. "How many lawyers does it take to change a lightbulb?"

"You told me that one the other day."

"No, this is a new one."

"All right. I'll go for it. So how many lawyers does it take to change a lightbulb?"

"It depends on how much money you want to spend." Candace grinned.

Mary groaned. "Bobby's a shoo-in to win the grand prize."

Laughing, Candace sorted through the tray of dried leaves to find one to add to her wreath. "Fortunately, Brad doesn't have to make his living telling jokes."

Mary's phone jangled, startling her. She reached around to the denim bag fastened to her wheelchair and pulled out her cell phone, flipping it open. It was Henry calling.

"Did you catch him?" she asked.

"Robb Phair just boarded the ferry for Friday Harbor," Henry told her. "Apparently he's done working for today. Artie's still at your house. It's all quiet there."

Mary's shoulders sagged. "Then Phair isn't the thief?"

"Either that or he's onto us. Or maybe Jade hasn't had a chance to tell him about the increased insurance coverage after all."

"How disappointing."

"Yeah, it is."

Mary heard the weariness in his voice. "So it's all right for me to go home now?"

"I've asked Artie to stick around there for another half hour, just to be on the safe side. After that, it should be clear for you to head home. But keep the doors locked."

Mary promised she would. But the fact that they hadn't caught the criminal yet would give her another sleepless night.

Except for adding some dried wildflowers to the wreath, she finished that task and drove home. Her nerves on edge, she pressed the remote to open the garage door. Everything looked normal as she went inside. The house felt empty. Even so, she checked every downstairs room, even looking under her craft table and having Finnegan check under her bed.

There was no way she could check upstairs. She'd simply have to pray no thief was lurking up there. She comforted herself with the thought that Finnegan showed no sign that an intruder was in the house.

Deciding a cup of tea might calm her, she headed back to the living room. That's when she heard a knock on the door.

Air lodged in her lungs. Maybe Phair hadn't gotten on the ferry after all. Or perhaps one of the other young men was the actual thief.

She peered around the corner from the dining room into the kitchen. Someone wearing a ball cap stood silhouetted outside the door. Someone short, she realized.

Bobby!

Relief swamped her and she wheeled to the door. "Bobby, is that you?"

"Yeah, it's me. I need some more help writing jokes."

Shaking her head and stifling a nervous laugh, she opened the door. "I'm afraid I'm not in a funny mood right now."

He went directly to the kitchen table and put his notebook down. "That's okay. Mom says I tickle her funny bone. I can tickle yours too."

He looked so bright and happy; perhaps he could at least get her mind off her problems.

"All right, tickle away."

He flipped open his notebook. "I thought I'd do something about being an only child."

"That's a very special thing, being an only child."

"Well, sure, but it means my parents put all their eggs in one basket and only one of 'em hatched. They've got a lot riding on me."

Mary took a plate from the cupboard and put some cookies on it. It looked like Artie Washburn had enjoyed several during his stay in the house. He'd washed out his coffee cup and left it in the draining rack to dry.

"See, if I mess up, they don't get a second chance. How are they gonna explain that to their grandkids?"

"I can see that would be a problem." She put the plate on the table. "Milk?"

"Sure. Thanks." Picking out a chocolate chip cookie, he took a big bite. "Besides, it's tough being an only child. If I get in trouble, I can't point at my little sister and say she did it. It's even tougher to blame an imaginary friend. My folks are smarter than that."

Amused, Mary put on some hot water to boil, poured Bobby's milk and joined him at the table.

"But I think I've got it figured out."

"Really?"

"Yep, I'm gonna clone myself. Whatever goes wrong, it'll always be the other guy's fault."

She sputtered a laugh. She wasn't sure the world was ready for two Bobby McDonalds, but what a joy he was to her. *Thank you, Lord.*

They worked together trying to create more jokes about being an only child until it was time for him to go home for dinner. Soon after that, Abby arrived home and learned that no one had attempted to rob the house.

"Poor Henry sounded so discouraged on the phone," Mary said.

"So am I." Abby washed her hands at the sink where Mary had been preparing veal patties for their dinner. "Maybe our thief isn't as greedy as we thought he was."

The doorbell rang, and Abby went to see who was there. A moment later, Abby was back in the kitchen, Henry right behind her. His tie was loose at his collar, and he looked weary.

"Looks like our thief outsmarted us this time," he said.

"Oh no. What happened?"

"When Candace Grover got home after work, she found someone had broken into her cottage, half trashing the place in the process. He got her computer, about fifty dollars she had on hand and an authentic Salish basket she bought about a year ago."

"The poor dear," Mary said. "She told me about that basket this afternoon."

"Did she have it insured?" Abby asked.

"No, she didn't want to pay the extra premium. Tucker quoted her more than she wanted to pay." He sat down heavily in one of the kitchen chairs.

"So Candace wasn't on the client list Tucker gave you of those with riders covering antiquities," Abby said. Tucker did, however, know about the basket. And so might others who had access to his office.

"That's right," Henry said. "Clearly, I missed something. I've gone back over my notes, and the only thing I can figure is that I didn't follow up on Naomi Yardley's friend and her son. If he was the one who snatched Naomi's cell phone . . . it's a thread I didn't follow. It might not even be connected to this current robbery." He shrugged. "Even so, it's the only lead I haven't tracked down. I'm going to Friday Harbor tomorrow morning to see what I can find out."

Abby sat down opposite him. "I'd like to go with you."

He nodded his approval but not with a lot of enthusiasm. "At this point, I need all the help I can get to nail this thief. We'll leave on the seven o'clock ferry."

"I think I should go into the shop tomorrow," Mary said. "I

know Candace will be upset, and Fridays are always a bit hectic. But I don't know about leaving the house empty. Do you think it will be safe, Henry?"

"At this point, I can't promise anything. I will have my deputy patrol by here more frequently than usual. But one of my men is out sick, and they've all been working overtime. I can't spare anyone to stay here at the house."

Mary understood. "I think I'll make it a point to get home as early in the afternoon as I can and leave the rest up to the Lord."

CHAPTER ✤ FIFTEEN

E ARLY THE NEXT MORNING, Abby parked her car in the ferry parking lot and walked over to Henry's tan police cruiser where he was in a line of vehicles waiting to board. The cool air felt fresh on her face, and the weatherman was predicting clear skies. Abby was hopeful spring was truly on the way now.

The incoming ferry had already docked as she slid into the passenger seat beside Henry. Dressed in his uniform with a for-est-green jacket, he looked grim enough to arrest every passenger on the ferry for loitering if they didn't get out of his way quickly enough.

Abby had chosen to dress professionally too, though she didn't wear a utility belt with a gun and handcuffs. Instead she wore a navy-blue pants suit and white blouse, the only decoration a golden eagle lapel pin with fierce outstretched claws. She was ready to snare someone too.

"Did you have time for breakfast?" she asked.

"I'll get something to eat onboard."

"I ate a muffin at home, but I'll join you for coffee." The onboard food service wasn't elegant by any means, but it served its purpose for travelers and those who had to depart home early.

The arriving vehicles began spilling out of the belly of the ferry. They drove up the ramp, then split off into town or out toward Primrose Lane and the east side of the island. Abby caught a glimpse of Dorthea Gilmore driving a car and wondered what mischief she'd get into today. The woman seemed determined to irritate half the population of Green Harbor.

When the arriving cars had all exited the ferry, the crewman signaled it was time for those heading to Friday Harbor to drive on board. Starting his engine, Henry followed a small pickup truck onto the ferry.

Henry had breakfast while Abby sipped a cup of coffee. About an hour later, the ferry arrived at Friday Harbor. Then the passengers reversed the boarding process, driving off the ferry and up into a town quite a bit larger than Green Harbor.

"I've got the Spauldings' address," Henry said. "We'll start there."

Once out of the town proper, he wound their way through narrow residential streets and finally to a cul de sac on one of the island's peninsulas that jutted out into the straits. He pulled over in front of a modest stucco house that was sure to have a terrific view.

Geri Spaulding answered the door. A slender woman with slightly graying hair glanced from Henry to Abby and back again.

Henry introduced himself and Abby, adding, "We're friends of Naomi Yardley."

Her hand flew to her throat. "Oh my, has something happened to her?"

"No, not at all," Abby quickly assured her. "Naomi's fine."

"We understand Naomi lost her cell phone while she was visiting you." Henry looked past Mrs. Spaulding into the house. "May we come in?"

"Of course." With a concerned expression, she backed away from the door to let them enter. "I've looked everywhere I could think of, but it hasn't turned up yet."

Henry walked into the living room and Abby followed. As she had expected, the view of the ocean was spectacular through the large picture window. Sun glistened off the straits, creating flashing diamonds of light.

Once in the center of the room, Henry turned to Mrs. Spaulding. "Is it possible your son could have picked it up? Perhaps accidentally?"

"Chuck?" Geri looked at him in surprise. "He has a phone of his own. Like most young people these days, he has it stuck to his ear every waking moment. We have to insist he turn it off during meals. What few meals he eats at home, at least," she added.

Abby guessed that was pretty typical of young people in their twenties. Independence was a heady thing.

"Naomi's phone has been implicated in a robbery on Lopez Island," Henry told Geri.

"Oh my. I had no idea."

"In the off chance he might have picked up the phone, would you mind if we take a look in his room?" Henry's casual stance belied the fact that he was, by the nature of his job and his uniform, an intimidating figure.

"His room's probably a mess. I don't go in there anymore. He's an adult and can take care of his own things."

"That's not a problem. We'll take a look and then get out of your hair." Henry gestured that she should lead the way to Chuck's room. Obviously uncertain what she should do, the boy's mother finally relented.

The bedroom reflected an odd mix of Chuck's youthful endeavors—a shelf full of football and baseball trophies—and his more adult interests—posters of monster trucks in danger of falling down steep cliffs.

Henry pulled on a pair of latex gloves and began searching through dresser drawers. Abby decided she had a few questions of her own.

"Does your son date much?" she asked.

"Some. He doesn't have a steady girl." Geri kept a careful eye on what Henry was up to. "I think Chuck would rather hang out with the guys he went to high school with and get his hands dirty tearing apart old trucks."

"Has he ever dated a girl who lives on Sparrow Island?"

"I, um, don't remember. Maybe in high school."

"Do you recall her name?"

"That was so long ago. Maybe Crystal? Something like that."

"Could her name have been Jade?"

Frowning, Geri hesitated. "Maybe. I simply don't recall."

Henry had moved on to the closet and was checking the top shelf, which was piled high with shoe boxes and board games.

"Most of those boxes are filled with the baseball cards he collected when he was younger," Geri told Henry as he opened a Nike box.

Abby eased over to a cluttered desk, studying a photograph of a young man with dark hair wearing a football uniform, his helmet in his hand. "Is this Chuck?"

Mrs. Spaulding glanced toward the photo. "Yes, he played quarterback and wide receiver in high school."

"You must have been very proud of him."

She shook her head. "I hated him playing football. I was terrified he'd be hurt, but he wouldn't hear of quitting. Then he did break his leg and had to have a knee replacement too. The surgery didn't heal right and he still walks with a limp. I think that's why he got into the monster truck thing. He can still be bigger and badder than anybody else."

"I'm so sorry, Mrs. Spaulding," Abby said gently. Surely Mary would have noticed if the thief had a limp.

A few minutes later, Henry finished searching the room. He settled his hat squarely on his head.

"I appreciate your letting me look around, Mrs. Spaulding."

"That's it?" she asked.

"I'll get back to you if I have any more questions. Thank you for your time." He reached the front door and stopped. "One more thing. Where's your son now?"

"He's working. Doan's Auto Garage downtown. He mostly works on specialty cars and big trucks. They tell me he's a talented mechanic."

Hearing a note of both pride and wistfulness, Abby gave her a reassuring smile.

Henry touched the brim of his hat and they walked back to the police cruiser.

"Did you find anything?" Abby asked.

"A couple of things he might not want his mother to know

about, but other than that—" He shrugged. "I don't think he's our guy."

"Neither do I."

"We'll go talk to the kid. But I'm afraid we're back to square one. Again."

Henry put the car in gear and made a U-turn. They'd gone a half block when his cell phone rang. He pulled over to the curb and answered.

"Sergeant Cobb." He listened, nodding, then lifted his head in obvious surprise. "A woman?" A few moments later, he snapped the phone closed.

"Looks like they've recovered Opal Collins' silver coffee and tea set," he said.

"That's wonderful. She'll be so pleased. Where did it turn up?"

"At a pawn shop in Olympia, of all places. The pawnbroker claims he just got around to reading the notice we sent out about stolen property. More likely a local cop was checking up on him because he has a history of dealing in stolen property."

Olympia, the capital of Washington State, was a long way from Sparrow Island. "Did he say who pawned the set?"

"A woman. He didn't give us much of a description— middle-aged, dark hair, no distinguishing features. Claimed her name was Mary Smith and that she'd inherited the silver set from her mother."

Abby leaned her head back against the headrest. "Where on earth does a middle-aged woman fit into this scheme?"

"I don't know. We've been looking at Jade as the connection. She sure wouldn't be mistaken for someone middle aged, and I checked her police record. She's clean. What about her mother?"

"The family's lived on Sparrow Island for at least fifteen years. Jade went to school here, moved away and returned a year or two ago. I can't imagine her mother is involved in anything illegal." Mentally trying to make sense of what they'd just learned, Abby took off her glasses and cleaned them with a soft cloth. "Chuck's mother thought he'd once dated a girl from Sparrow Island. She thought the girl's name was Crystal but wasn't sure. I suppose it could have been Jade, but that doesn't explain how Jade's mother would fit in. Mrs. Spaulding matches that pawnbroker's general description, but that doesn't fit either."

"Nothing about this case fits." He shifted into gear again. "Let's go see what Chuck has to say for himself."

TWO HOURS LATER, Abby was back in her own car on Sparrow Island driving to the Nature Museum. Based on his time cards at Doan's Auto Garage, Chuck had an alibi for all but one of the robberies. His limp was also so pronounced, Mary wouldn't have missed it.

Discouraged, Abby drove into the parking lot. The sunny day had brought more visitors to the conservatory than earlier in the week, the increased number of cars evidence that many had decided to stroll through the grounds.

Inside she discovered several families had gathered around the terrarium with the pupae display. Hugo was there as well.

"We have butterflies!" He announced proudly.

Abby moved up close to get a good look at the new arrivals. Sure enough, three small butterflies sat perched on the cabbage leaves, their respective chrysalises discarded. The upper side of the butterflies' wings had black tips. Two of the butterflies had black spots in the center of their forewings.

She had to admit she'd hoped the butterflies would emerge as colorful creatures, like monarch butterflies, but these three made up for their plain appearance with their incredible delicacy.

The families observing the butterflies seemed to be equally enamored of the tiny beauties.

"Do you know what kind of butterflies they are?" she asked Hugo.

"Oh, I've known all along." He smiled smugly.

"Well?"

"The answer is actually quite obvious if you think about it."

After her morning with Henry and her frustration with not being able to solve the robberies, she didn't want to think. "It would be easier if you just told me."

"Yes, do," a woman standing next to him said.

He opened his mouth, about to do just that, when Bobby came racing into the museum.

"Did they emerge?"

"They did indeed, young man," Hugo said, standing back so Bobby could get a good look of the terrarium.

"Cool! I saw two butterflies at school. I was sure my butter-flies had probably emerged too." His grin was huge and as proud as Hugo's. "I know what they are!"

"Would one of you please enlighten the rest of us," Abby pleaded.

Hugo deferred to Bobby.

"It's easy. I found a picture of them in a book at the library.

They're small cabbage white butterflies. The ones with the spots are girls."

"Well done, young man!" Hugo gave Bobby a high five.

The adults standing nearby were duly impressed by Bobby's knowledge.

"There're also large whites, but the small ones are more common," Bobby told them.

"Cabbage butterflies," Abby muttered. "Obvious. But only if you're aware there is such a butterfly." She picked up the ballot box stuffed with guesses made by museum visitors. "Guess we'll have to see how many winners we have and send them a certificate."

Hugo held up his hand to stop her from leaving. "Wait just a minute. I have another joke for you."

"Another knock-knock joke?" Not exactly what she needed at the moment.

"No, no, this is something quite different."

"Go ahead, Mr. Baron," Bobby said. "I wanna hear your joke."

"Good lad." Hugo winked at the boy. "All right then, what do moths learn at school?"

Bobby giggled. "I don't know, Mr. Baron. What do moths learn in school?"

"They learn *mothmatics*!"

Bobby giggled again. The very young children standing nearby didn't get it, but their parents did and laughed politely.

Abby suppressed a groan. "Aren't you out of school early today, Bobby?"

"Yeah, it was a short day."

"Ah, I see." She smiled at those around her. "Well, if you'll excuse me, I've got to get to work. Enjoy your visit."

"When are we going to release the butterflies?" Bobby asked.

"Oh, well . . . Why don't we give them a couple of days here so our visitors can enjoy them? We can release them Sunday afternoon. How does that sound?"

"Great! I'll be here."

As she turned to head for her office, her cell phone rang. Fumbling with the box of ballots, she retrieved her phone from her pocket and checked the caller ID. Not recognizing the number, she frowned. So few people had this number . . .

"Dr. Stanton," she answered formally.

"Abby, it's Mollie Berman."

The school bus driver's calling gave Abby a jolt. "Yes, Mollie, what is it?"

"You said to call if I saw anything out of the ordinary. Actually, I tried calling Mary at home, but I didn't get an answer."

Abby glanced at her watch. Two thirty. "She's probably still at Island Blooms. Is there something wrong?"

"I don't know." The sound of youthful voices could be heard in the background. "I wondered if you and Mary were having some work done around the house?"

"Work done?" Worried now, Abby handed the ballot box to Hugo.

"Yeah, you know. Some repair work or remodeling. I just drove by and there's a white pickup truck parked out front. I saw the driver walk around toward the back of the house. I dunno. It just seemed strange, then I remembered I'd seen that same truck near Opal Collins' house the day of her robbery."

Darren Barber! The young man working at the marina. A man with a police record.

"Dial 911, Mollie. Tell dispatch you think Mary's house is being robbed. And tell them I'm on my way there right now." She snapped the phone shut. Her gaze met Hugo's.

"I'm coming with you." He handed the ballot box to Bobby.

There wasn't time to argue. She raced out the door to her car, Hugo matching her stride for stride.

CHAPTER ✾ SIXTEEN

ABBY MADE IT HOME IN under ten minutes. Skidding to a stop in front of the pickup truck, she hopped out of the car. Hugo did the same. Lumber filled the truck bed and there was a locked tool box. A workman's truck. A man with a purpose. Perfect cover for a robbery.

Artie Washburn was already on the scene, the light bar on his police cruiser silently flashing red and yellow. His gun drawn, he crept cautiously toward the back of the house. He glanced toward Abby and Hugo, signaling them to stay put.

From where Abby stood, the wailing burglar alarm on the scrimshaw cabinet sliced through the air like a serrated knife, jagged and painful even at a distance. No neighbors were home to hear the siren. Darren Barber thought he had free reign to steal the scrimshaw collection. If not for Mollie's alertness, he would have gotten away with it.

Indignation knotted in Abby's stomach. That thief had violated Mary's sense of security and made all the victims feel vulnerable.

She'd been so sure Robb Phair was the guilty party. Not so.

Instinctively, her hands balled into fists. She wanted to personally confront the young man who had done so much to hurt so many. All because of greed.

She started to take a step forward, but Hugo restrained her.

"Easy does it," he said. "Let the deputy handle this. It's his job."

Abby knew Hugo was right. She had no weapon to either defend herself or to stop Darren. But Artie had vanished along the side of the house minutes ago. What was happening? Why wasn't Henry or another deputy here to back up Artie?

A weapon! That's what she needed.

Quickly she went to the back of her car and popped the hatch. She always carried a heavy-duty flashlight to use in an emergency. It weighed as much as a billy club and could serve the same purpose.

"What do you think you're doing?" Hugo asked.

"I want to be ready if the thief gets past Artie."

"Put that thing away." Hugo tried to take it from her. "You're the one who'll get hurt."

She had no intention of getting hurt or being defenseless. She wrenched the flashlight away from Hugo.

Just then she realized the alarm had stopped wailing. A male voice yelled something inside the house. Simultaneously, Mary's van roared into the driveway and the front door of the house flew open.

A man dressed in a dark jacket, cap and pants came racing out. As she'd expected, Abby recognized the thief as Darren Barber, although his hair looked shorter than when she'd met him at the marina. He carried a heavy duffle bag in one hand.

The scrimshaw collection!

"Darren!" Abby broke into a run, angling to intercept him before he got to his truck. She held the flashlight at the ready to deliver the strongest blow she could.

Hugo shouted, "Come back!"

A flash of golden-brown fur raced toward Darren on a collision course. Finnegan leapt into the air, crashing into Darren chest high and knocking the thief to the ground, sending the duffle bag thudding onto the lawn. The dog stood over the downed man, lips pulled back in a snarl, a growl rumbling in his chest.

"Get him away from me!" Scooting along on his back, Darren tried to escape from Finnegan, but the dog stayed right with him. Exertion made Darren cough, a deep, heavy sound like Abby had heard on Opal's recording.

Abby didn't doubt for a minute that Finnegan remembered this was the man who had broken into his mistress's house two weeks ago. He wasn't about to let Darren get away this time.

But why did Finnegan growl at Robb Phair at the sheriff's substation? she thought.

Gun in hand, Artie came out of the house at a run. "On your stomach! Put your hands behind your head. Now!"

"Get the dog—"

"Do it now!" Artie ordered again.

When the man complied, Artie approached him from the rear. "Mary, call off your dog."

"Finnegan, come!"

For once, Finnegan didn't instantly obey her command, and Mary, who had exited her van, had to repeat the order.

With Finnegan safely at Mary's side, Artie holstered his gun. He snapped a cuff on one of Darren's wrists, twisted his arm behind him and captured the other arm to cuff it too.

Then he dragged the thief to his feet, forced him to the patrol car and had him bend over the hood with his feet wide apart. In control of the situation, Artie patted Darren down. As a final step, he shoved the young man into the backseat of the police vehicle, slamming the door shut behind him.

Only then did Abby exhale in relief.

"Everyone all right?" Artie asked when Darren was safely inside the cruiser.

"We're fine, thanks to you," Hugo said.

Artie slipped into the cruiser and used the radio to report the situation to the substation.

Stepping out of the car again, Artie said, "Next time, you civilians ought to stay out of the way. You could have been hurt or taken as a hostage."

Abby hadn't considered the hostage possibility, which would have escalated the situation and made things more difficult for Artie. "Let's hope there isn't any next time."

Mary made her way to the duffle bag left on the ground. "Is the scrimshaw collection in this bag?"

"I imagine so, Mrs. Reynolds," Artie said.

"Can I put the pieces back where they belong?"

"Not right now. The bag and its contents are evidence. I'm sure the sarge will get your things back to you as soon as he can."

Visibly yearning to hold the contents of the bag in her hands again, Mary nodded her agreement.

"It'll be all right," Abby told her sister. She rested a reassuring hand on Mary's shoulder.

"I know. It's just that . . . Jacob would be so upset. If that young man has broken any of . . ." She shook her head as though to deny the possibility.

A second police cruiser arrived, lights flashing. Henry got out of the car and quickly scanned the scene.

"Was he working alone?" he asked his deputy.

"I haven't had a chance to clear the house, but I think so."

"You stay with the prisoner. I'll take care of it." As he headed toward the front door, he gave Mary a concerned look and unholstered his weapon. "You okay?"

"I'm fine. Be careful."

When he vanished through the open door, Abby said, "Mary, how did you know the house was being robbed?"

"Mollie called me at the shop. She said she'd already called you and 911, but thought I'd want to know too."

"We're fortunate she was so observant, or Darren would have gotten away with the entire collection."

"Speaking of being fortunate," Hugo said, "Finnegan certainly knew what to do. I was unaware he'd been trained as an attack dog."

"He hasn't been." Leaning over, she gave Finnegan a hug. "But I think he can count on having a nice juicy bone with his dinner tonight."

WHEN THE EXCITEMENT had simmered down, Abby drove Hugo back to the museum and dropped him off. She wanted to hear what Darren had to say. It was obvious he was getting information from someone about where to find valuable artifacts. She was still betting on Jade as his coconspirator, but was anxious to hear the truth from his own lips. She suspected when Jade told them Darren was a loser, she'd intended to divert attention from herself.

When Abby arrived at the sheriff's substation, she discovered William Jansen was already there looking as excited as a man who'd just been told he held a winning lottery ticket. His tie hung crookedly and his suit jacket was buttoned wrong as though he'd left his office in a hurry.

"Did you hear the news? They caught the Sparrow Island thief red-handed. I heard it on the police frequency. Big news, huh? Problem is, nobody'll give me a statement. Henry's stonewalling me and his deputies have all gone deaf and dumb."

She glanced at Mike Bennett, who was working behind the counter and ignoring William's overly loud protests.

"I'm sure Henry will give you a statement when he's sorted things out."

"They won't even give me the name of the guy. I could be rounding up background information. You know, flesh out the story about his criminal record if he's got one. Where he was born and raised." He cocked his head. "Say, I bet you know something about the guy they caught. The break-in was at your house."

"No comment, William. Sorry."

"Ah, give me a break, huh? The public has a right to know. Is the guy local? You can give me a hint, can't you?"

She looked to Mike Bennett in the hope he'd rescue her from William's persistent questions. Detecting no reaction to her silent plea for help, she decided she'd have to send a clearer SOS.

"Mike, would you please tell Henry I'd like to see him."

William objected. "Wait a minute. I was here first."

The deputy looked uncertain. "Let me check, Dr. Stanton."

Abby waited. William fumed. Finally the deputy allowed Abby to enter the inner sanctum while William sputtered and turned red in the face.

She walked past the interrogation room. Slouched in a chair, Darren was all alone.

Abby continued on to Henry's office.

"Has Darren confessed?" she asked from the doorway.

"Nope. He asked for an attorney and clammed up tighter than a drum. I'll have another go at him after the boys in Friday Harbor execute the search warrant the judge issued for Darren's apartment. By then we ought to have someone appointed as a public defender here for the kid."

"We caught him red-handed. Seems like he'd be better off to confess everything and tell us where the stolen property's gone. Wouldn't a court go easier on him?"

Henry tipped back in his chair and locked his hands behind his head. "I know that, but this youngster has mush for brains. Or maybe he's watched too many TV shows. In any case, he's not talking."

"So he hasn't implicated Jade?"

"Nary a hint."

Shaking her head, she stepped into the office and took the chair in front of Henry's desk. "I'd been so sure Robb Phair was guilty, particularly after Finnegan growled at Robb when he was taken into interrogation."

"Yep, I was leaning that way too. We'll never know for sure, but I'm guessing Finnegan could smell Darren's scent when the door opened to the lineup room. That's what he was reacting to."

That made sense to Abby, but the dog's response had certainly misled them.

"Mary hadn't picked Darren out of the lineup either," Abby said.

"Lineups and eye witnesses aren't always reliable. That's why we do our best to come up with evidence that can't be disputed."

"Like catching a thief in the act."

He acknowledged a jury would find that pretty convincing evidence.

Henry's phone rang. He answered and jotted down notes on a yellow pad while he talked with the caller.

"That was the detective in Friday Harbor," he said after he hung up. "We've got the right man. They found two of the stolen computers in Barber's apartment and a nice stash of cash, which won't be traceable. They also found Jade's e-mail address in his personal computer but no recent contact. They're getting his phone records now."

"He was foolish not to get rid of the stolen computers."

"Maybe he didn't know where to pawn them."

"Except some middle-aged woman figured out what to do with Opal's silver tea and coffee service."

He scratched his fringe of gray hair. "And we haven't figured out who she is or how she connects to all this."

Shoving back from his desk, Henry stood. "I'm going to have Artie bring Jade Kebby in for questioning. Maybe she'll be a little more talkative than Darren."

A HALF HOUR LATER, Abby decided Jade wasn't a talker. She was a screamer.

"I didn't tell Darren a thing! He's a total loser. He'd be the last person on earth I'd talk to about Mr. Billings' clients. I'd lose my job." Agitated, she paced around the interrogation room, arms waving, finger pointing, while Henry sat calmly watching her act. If that's what it was.

"If you didn't tell Darren about the insured artifacts, who do you think did?" Henry asked.

"How should I know? I just do my job. I don't go nosing into my boss's business."

"Do you have reason to think Mr. Billings might have told Darren what to look for and where?"

The girl rolled her eyes. "Mr. Billings is a regular do-gooder Boy Scout. He'd never have anything to do with Darren."

"Darren has your e-mail address."

Whirling, she glowered at Henry. "That doesn't mean I e-mail back. I'm telling you, he's a jerk. If he stole all those antiques, then he belongs in jail. Not me!"

Abby didn't think Jade was a particularly pleasant young woman. But if her anger was legitimate—if she wasn't guilty of anything—she had a right to be upset.

Patiently, Henry took Jade through her entire history with Darren. Where they'd met. How many times they'd gone out. Where they had gone. Had he ever come to the office to see her? Had he ever been left alone in the office while she stepped out?

"No, no never!" she insisted.

"Would you let one of my men search your house?" Henry asked.

"Search till you're blue in the face, for all I care." She threw up her arms in dismay. "You aren't going to find anything. All you're going to do is upset my mother."

Excusing himself, Henry left her alone in the interrogation room, still pacing and waving her arms.

"Now that's a real drama queen if I ever met one," he commented to Abby.

"Do you think it's an act?"

"I don't know. I'll send her home with Artie, see what he can find."

"You could put Jade and Darren in the same room together and see what happens."

A smile twitched the corners of his lips. "You're a devious woman, Dr. Stanton."

Unfortunately, her devious idea nearly cost Darren his eyesight when Jade attacked him with her long fingernails the moment he was brought into the interrogation room. Henry and Artie had to break up the fight, which earned them a few bruises too.

To add to the difficulty, the public defender notified Henry that he was in court and couldn't get to Sparrow Island until the next day. Darren would have to spend the night in a Sparrow Island jail cell.

Concluding she'd learn nothing more until Darren decided to talk, Abby headed home, leaving the substation via the back door. She wanted to avoid William and the questions he was sure to ask.

She'd let Henry handle the press.

CHAPTER ❦ SEVENTEEN

THE CLOUDLESS MORNING with the sun just stroking the treetops with gold made for a perfect beginning for the last day of the workweek.

Blossom joined Abby on the back deck while she read her daily devotions. Knowing Darren was safely locked up in jail had made for a good night's sleep and Abby felt relaxed for the first time in days.

She'd feel even better, of course, if Darren would tell Henry who was feeding him information about the artifacts he'd stolen and where they were now.

Finishing her devotional reading, she said a quick prayer of thanks and went inside. Blossom followed her into the kitchen where Mary was sitting at the table.

"After all the excitement yesterday, how are you feeling?" Abby asked, refilling her coffee mug.

"I'm fine, except that Jacob's scrimshaw cabinet looks so empty."

"I'm sure Henry will return the collection as soon as he can."

"I know. Still . . . oh, with all that went on yesterday, I forgot to tell you that Richard Decker called me on my cell while I was at the shop. He apologized for taking so long, but he's come up with the name of a dealer of Native American antiquities whose reputation is somewhat suspect." She reached into her denim bag and pulled out a slip of paper. "His name's Sylvester Dominic and he has an antiques store near Seattle."

Taking the note, Abby glanced at the name and address. "I'll take this to Henry. He'll want to check this dealer out, see if he's the one fencing the stolen goods." That might not be easy. The authorities couldn't simply pop in on a businessman and start accusing him of committing a felony.

As Abby slipped the note into her jacket pocket, she had another thought. "It would be interesting to find out if this Dominic person has any connection to Tucker. The insurance angle has to be how Darren knew where to find antiquities."

No question, to get to the bottom of this mystery would be like untangling a skein of Mary's yarn.

She found a bran muffin for breakfast and poured herself some juice. She'd stop by the sheriff's substation on her way to work.

By the time she finished her breakfast and had driven into town, the public defender had arrived at the station house and was talking with Darren.

"Don't you wish you could hear what they're saying?" she said to Henry as they stood outside the interrogation room.

"Nope. It's against the law to eavesdrop on an attorney and his client. Besides, I've got Darren dead to rights. I don't want to jeopardize my case against him by doing anything illegal.

We'll be taking the kid to Friday Harbor for arraignment when the lawyer's done with him."

A true man of the law, Abby thought. "I've got some additional information for you." She handed him Mary's note. "It's the name of the antique dealer Richard Decker thinks might be unscrupulous enough to handle stolen merchandise. Sylvester Dominic."

Thoughtfully, Henry walked back toward his office. "I'll have the detective in Friday Harbor check Darren's computer and his phone records, see if they've been in contact. Even that may not produce anything since he's been using throwaway or stolen phones. It also strikes me as a long shot that Darren would know where to find a high-end antique dealer. If he refuses to talk, I'm pretty much at a dead end."

"At least the robberies will stop now that you have him locked up."

"But the brains behind the operation are still out there somewhere. That's who we have to focus on now."

"Do you think, assuming Dominic's at the bottom of the robberies, that he'll go underground now that Darren's been caught?"

"I think if we're going to nail whoever's behind the break-ins, we'd better do it in a hurry before they have time to hop a plane to Brazil or somewhere else that doesn't have an extradition treaty with us. And remember, if Dominic's our man, we have no idea how he's connected to Tucker or how he knew about the antiquities that Tucker insured."

For now, Abby just had to accept that there were lots of loose ends.

After she left Henry, Abby intended to go on to the Nature Museum. She still had to make up the certificates for those who had guessed correctly about the white cabbage butterflies and mail them out. She also needed to think through whether the conservatory should organize a bird inventory on nearby uninhabited islands. It would be a big project and expensive. She'd have to find a sponsor to underwrite the program—not an easy task to accomplish.

Instead of going to work, almost as though her hybrid car had a mind of its own, she found herself parking in front of Tucker Billings' office.

She walked up to the door and let herself in. Jade wasn't at her desk. She walked to Tucker's open office door and was about to knock when she let out an audible gasp.

Tucker and Dorthea were standing by his desk kissing.

Tucker looked up, surprised by Abby's arrival.

"I'm so sorry," Abby said. Embarrassed heat flooded her cheeks. "I didn't realize . . . Jade isn't here. . . ."

Tucker and Dorthea quickly stepped apart, Dorthea appearing far less disconcerted by Abby's untimely arrival than Abby was. In fact, she looked quite smug.

"It's all right." Dorthea smoothed her hair and straightened her tailored blouse. "I was just leaving." She turned back and whispered something to Tucker, which caused him to blush. Then she sauntered out of the office.

"I'm truly sorry, Tucker. It never occurred to me—"

He waved off her apology and cleared his throat. "Nothing to be sorry for. Jade called in sick this morning." As he walked behind his desk, he adjusted his tie and buttoned his jacket. "Was there something you wanted to see me about?"

"I had just one quick question," she said. "I probably should have called you." She certainly hadn't planned to interrupt his tête-à-tête with Dorthea. As far as she knew, they were both unmarried and were free to pursue romance with anyone they chose. Picturing them as a couple was a little jarring, however, even though she'd seen them walking out of the town council meeting together. Dorthea didn't seem his type.

"What's the question?" he asked.

"Does the name Sylvester Dominic mean anything to you?" She watched for his reaction, but he simply shook his head.

"I'm afraid it doesn't ring a bell. Am I supposed to know him?"

"I thought you might have come across him in your business dealings. He's an antique dealer." Again, Tucker appeared at a loss to recall the name.

"No, I don't think I've met the gentleman. He might have provided an insurance appraisal of property owned by one of my clients, but nothing comes to mind. I suppose I could go through my records, but that would take quite a bit of time. With Jade out ill . . ." He left the thought hanging.

Abby imagined the young woman was still upset about yesterday.

"No, checking all the files won't be necessary. It was only an off chance." Assuming Dominic was fencing the stolen property, she didn't want to send up too many red flags until Henry had a chance to check the man out.

As gracefully as she could, she apologized again for having interrupted his morning and escaped to her car.

It takes all kinds, she reminded herself as she drove to the conservatory and went to her desk. Trying to get Dorthea and Tucker out of her mind, she focused on the butterfly identification certificates until about noon, when Henry called.

"The cops in Seattle think taking a look at this antique dealer Dominic is a good bet," he said. "They've had him on their radar for some shady deals, but they haven't been able to prove anything."

"Then you're going to get a search warrant for his property and records?"

"Nope. The Seattle boys have tried that and came up empty. We're going to have to send someone in undercover with a wire, see if we can get enough incriminating evidence on tape so a judge will issue another warrant."

"You mean have him confess to handling stolen merchandise? Who will you send in? If Dominic's dealing with high-end stolen property, he'd make one of your deputies as a cop in a nanosecond. Apparently he's already dodged the Seattle police."

"We'll use a couple of Seattle undercover officers, probably from the narcotics or gang enforcement units."

"That'll never work. Whoever goes undercover needs to be sophisticated, knowledgeable about antiques and appear wealthy enough to be a legitimate buyer. It should be someone like—" She halted abruptly as the idea struck her. "Hugo Baron and I should be the ones to go undercover."

Henry coughed as though he'd choked on the thought. "I can't send you and Hugo into a potentially dangerous situation."

"But it's the perfect setup. Hugo's so smooth and so knowledgeable, no one would make him as an undercover police officer. And I certainly don't fit the mold either." Suddenly she was excited about the prospect of being in on the arrest of a dealer of stolen property. "This Dominic person would be wise to anything else."

"I don't know, Abby." She imagined Henry shaking his head in disapproval.

"This is our one best chance of nailing Dominic and

recovering the stolen merchandise," she argued. "I'm sure Hugo will be more than happy to go undercover in order to assure Dominic can be held accountable."

Several seconds of silence passed. "I'd have to be sure the Seattle police can protect you if anything went wrong. If you're in danger, we'd have to pull you out of there, even if it meant losing the chance to arrest Dominic."

"Understood."

"The guy's store is in a decent neighborhood. You'd both have to be wired up so we'll know if you're in any kind of trouble."

"Hugo and I can pull it off, I'm sure."

He hesitated again. "All right, it's worth a shot, but I'll have to clear it with the Seattle police," Henry said, still reluctant as he described the plan he had in mind. "If we can collar Dominic, we may be able to work backwards and spring a trap on whoever his contact is here on Sparrow Island. It has to be somebody bigger than Darren."

SATURDAY MORNING, Hugo picked up Abby in time to make the early ferry to Bellingham. Dressed in a navy-blue blazer with a white cravat and tan slacks, he looked for all the world to be a wealthy collector, the role he was playing for their sting operation. His snow-white hair and matching mustache added to his always distinguished appearance.

To pose as his wife, Abby had chosen a forest-green knit dress with long sleeves that she accessorized with a double strand of pearls and matching earrings. She'd bought the dress several years ago to wear to a tea honoring the president of Cornell University.

"You look spectacular, Abby." Standing in the front hallway, Hugo gave her an admiring look. "I've brought you a small item to assist us in carrying out our mission." From his pocket, he pulled out a small velvet box and opened it.

At the sight of a delicate gold wedding band, Abby's breath lodged in her throat. Her gaze flew up to Hugo's.

"It's quite all right, my dear. I'm sure Clarissa would say having you wear her wedding ring to help catch a crook is a worthy endeavor." He removed the ring from the box and slipped it on Abby's finger.

Goose flesh shimmered up her arm. "I hadn't thought about wearing a ring. I should have, of course, as part of our disguise."

"The ring matches mine, you see. I hadn't worn it in some time, but it still fits."

She heard residual grief in his voice and knew he must have been inconsolable when he lost his wife to malaria while they were traveling through Africa many years ago.

Abby closed her hand as though to hold the ring tightly. "I promise I'll take very good care of Clarissa's ring."

"I have no doubt of that. Shall we go, Mrs. Huntington?" Using the fictitious name the police had created for them as a wealthy married couple from New York, he offered his arm.

Struggling with an emotion she didn't quite understand, she hesitated an instant before taking his arm. "Yes, Mr. Huntington, let's be on our way."

THEY'D MET HENRY on the ferry, and he'd briefed them on the plan. In Seattle they met the lead detective on the case, Bill Costner. A lean, trim forty-year-old, he made sure Abby and Hugo were properly wired for sound.

"Are you sure you're going to be all right with this?" he asked them both.

"We'll be quite all right," Hugo assured them. "I am actually a collector of various native arts and crafts from around the world. So carrying off this charade should be simple."

Detective Costner didn't look a hundred percent convinced. "Dr. Stanton, we have no reason to believe Dominic might get violent or we wouldn't even consider using civilians. If at any time you feel threatened, either of you, get out of there. Do you understand?"

"Yes, sir. I'm quite confident Hugo and I can handle the situation." Abby mentally crossed her fingers.

The detective had then given them a tour through a van that was crammed full of electronic equipment, all the time reassuring them that plenty of plainclothes officers would be nearby to provide cover for them if anything went wrong.

A half hour later, as Hugo drove the rental car into the parking lot of Antiques Galore, Dominic's business, Abby found her palms damp with sweat and her mouth dry. Apparently, she wasn't as confident as she'd wanted Detective Costner to believe.

Located off of a secondary highway, the building looked like a former barn painted red, white and blue. On both sides of the steep roof, large white letters read SALE, as though there was a perpetual sale in progress.

Hugo angled into a parking slot on the asphalt lot and brought the car to a halt.

Nerves tightened a knot in Abby's stomach. Firmly, she told herself to relax. *Lord, please watch over us and keep us safe.*

Hugo helped her out of the car and they walked toward the

building. An old merry-go-round horse with a chipped ear sat outside the door along with a wooden barrel and a metal sewing manikin.

"This place looks pretty much like any antiques store I've been in, except larger," Abby commented, thinking the entrance, at least, conveyed a sense of decay and despair.

"It's all a front, apparently, for Dominic's real business, fencing stolen objets d'art."

The cavernous building smelled of dust and mold. The clutter of old jewelry, empty wooden spools for thread, children's toys, lamps, photos, oil paintings, furniture and other merchandise that belonged in a Goodwill store—at best—created a sense of claustrophobia.

A creepy sensation sped down Abby's spine, and she took a deep breath, nearly choking in the process.

A wrinkled, wizened old woman, who might have qualified as an antique herself, approached them. A black cardigan sweater hung limply from her bony shoulders.

"Hello, there. Looking for something in particular? Whatever it is, we have it somewhere."

His back ramrod straight, his nose lifted at a disdainful angle, Hugo said, "We'd like to speak with Mr. Dominic. Privately."

The woman blinked, then gave them both an assessing look. Apparently deciding they were worthy of Mr. Dominic's personal attention—or had enough money to be worthwhile customers—she nodded briskly. "One moment please."

She vanished into the back of the building.

As nearly as Abby could tell, she and Hugo were the only shoppers on this Saturday morning. Usually antique stores were crowded on weekends, mostly with lookers rather than buyers, she supposed. But somehow the crowds had not arrived at this off-the-beaten-track store.

And no sign of police officers either.

Shortly a stocky gentleman in a dark suit appeared from the back of the building. He walked toward them with a determined gait that announced he was a busy man, don't waste his time. He brusquely introduced himself. "You wanted to see me?"

"Hugo Huntington here. My wife Abigail." Hugo extended his hand. Dominic was forced to take it. Abby noted he wore gold rings on nearly every finger, most of them mounted with precious gems.

The antique business must be very profitable, she thought. *At least the way Dominic runs his company.*

"I'm a collector of native art and antiquities," Hugo said. "During our travels throughout the world, I've picked up bits and pieces, both to enjoy and as an investment."

"His Masai spear and shield are quite impressive," Abby added. "Although I was somewhat fearful for my life a time or two there."

Dominic was definitely paying attention now.

"While we've been traveling the Northwest," Hugo continued, "I've become quite enamored of authentic Native American antiquities. Not the commercial goods that are now being mass produced. Museum quality, if you please." Leaning toward Dominic and lowering his voice confidentially, Hugo said, "We've been told you have access to that type of merchandise."

Dominic glanced around the store. A man had entered after Abby and Hugo, and she hoped he was a plainclothes policeman.

"What you're describing can be quite expensive," Dominic said.

"Money is no object," Hugo replied. "Assuming the price is fair. I prefer dealing in cash, if that's acceptable to you."

Greed flared in the dealer's eyes and he was hooked. "Did you have anything special in mind?"

Abby spoke up. "I'm fond of the primitive quality of cedar carvings. Would anything like that be available?" Like Wilma Washburn's stolen ceremonial mask? she left unsaid.

"Her tastes tend toward the simple," Hugo said. "I'd actually favor a few pieces of scrimshaw, assuming the artwork is of high caliber."

The plan, as Henry had explained it, was to find out what Dominic had in his possession, buy it and then bait him by specifically suggesting they'd be willing to pay big bucks for scrimshaw art.

Again he scanned the store. "I may be able to help you. If you'd like to step into the back?"

He ushered them to back offices and then to a door marked EXIT, which he held open for them to step outside.

"Where are we going?" Abby asked. She hoped the police were listening. Leaving the premises with Dominic hadn't been part of the plan.

"I don't keep my high-quality pieces here, Mrs. Huntington. You can understand why not, I'm sure. But it's not far, I assure you."

Anxious, Abby glanced at Hugo, but his expression gave nothing away. He looked as calm and in control as he always did.

A brand new silver Mercedes was parked nearby. With a remote, Dominic unlocked the car.

"Perhaps we should take our own car, dear, and follow Mr. Dominic," Abby suggested sweetly, picturing a hostage situation like Artie Washburn had warned against.

Opening the back door of the car, Dominic indicated she should get in. She didn't dare balk at this point. He would become suspicious, and they'd lose their chance to catch him with the stolen property. She would have to play along.

After she was seated, the two men got into the front seat. The car was stiflingly hot from sitting in the sun. Perspiration dampened her face.

"I gather you have a second office," Hugo said casually.

Dominic started the car and drove out the back way. "A more private place in which to conduct my business. Who'd you say suggested I could help you?"

"I prefer to keep my sources confidential."

Dear Lord, help the police follow us. Abby forced herself not to look out the back window to check.

The car made a turn. Abby caught the street name. "Oh, we're on Oleander Street. Are all these streets named after flowers? That's very quaint." *I hope you heard that, Henry.*

Dominic glanced in the rearview mirror. "Most of the streets around Seattle are numbered. Not very inspired, I'm afraid."

He turned onto another street, a quasi-industrial area.

"I see what you mean," Abby said. "Two-hundred-and-forty-forth Street must be a long way from downtown."

Ignoring her comment, he pulled into a driveway alongside a one-story building and drove to the back of the property, out of sight of the street. No one was around, and there were no other cars in the lot.

After he parked, Dominic led them inside the building,

disarming an alarm system as they entered. For all Abby knew, they were about to be mugged, robbed and left for dead in this isolated place. Not a comforting thought.

She sent up another quick prayer. Next time she'd leave the police work to the professionals.

Dominic switched on a light.

The showroom was like none Abby had ever seen. Oil paintings decorated the walls. Diamond rings and necklaces glistened in glass display cases only slightly smaller than those used for the Crown Jewels in London. One entire display was devoted to Native American specimens of the highest quality. And there, just as she'd hoped, rested what must have been Wilma's precious cedar mask. Right next to it presumably was Opal Collins' sla-hal game.

While Dominic and Hugo negotiated a price, Abby studied the merchandise with care. She spotted what she supposed was Margaret Blackstock's Tlingit Indian rattle-top basket. And when she checked the paintings on the wall, she was sure Margaret's painting of Central Park was among them.

Everything in this room was stolen property!

The police hadn't known about this secret room. Now they would, assuming she and Hugo got out of here alive. Sylvester Dominic's days as a free man were nearly over.

Hugo concluded the transaction by handing Dominic the marked bills the police had provided.

Dominic quickly counted the money with his stubby, ring-encrusted fingers. "I believe I have a reliable source for some high-quality scrimshaw. When it arrives, I'll be happy to give you a call."

"It's a pleasure doing business with you, Mr. Dominic," Hugo said, shaking the man's hand.

Within minutes, they were back in the Antiques Galore parking lot and driving away. They'd arranged to meet Henry and the Seattle detectives a few miles down the road.

Abby leaned back against the headrest. "I've never been so scared in my life. My heart's still beating so hard, you can probably hear it."

Glancing in her direction, Hugo smiled. "Knock knock."

She groaned. "Not now."

"It'll get your mind off of our little adventure. Knock knock."

Defeated, she sighed. "Who's there?"

"Juicy."

"Oh, Hugo!" Despite everything, she laughed. "Juicy who?"

"Juicy what I saw?"

She shook her head. If open mic night didn't happen soon, she'd go crazy with all the jokes going around town. But she'd get even. She had a joke of her own.

"Knock knock," she said.

He lifted his brows. "Who's there?"

"Police."

He chuckled. "Police who?"

"Police stop telling those knock-knock jokes."

CHAPTER ❧ EIGHTEEN

When they returned to Sparrow Island that evening, Henry brought the scrimshaw collection back to Mary.

"We're going to use this as bait again," Henry told her while Abby arranged the pieces in the display cabinet. "Word will have gotten out that we caught Darren before he could get away with the scrimshaw. We're keeping him incommunicado at Friday Harbor. When Dominic makes contact with his source and says he's got a buyer, whoever it is, he won't be able to resist trying again for the collection. He'll either have to hire someone else to do the job, or do the break-in himself. I'm betting on the latter."

"I'm surprised Darren's attorney hasn't convinced the young man to turn state's evidence to get a lighter sentence," Mary said.

"That surprises me too." Abby arranged two large whale bones with exquisitely carved sailing vessels next to each other. "He must either be afraid of that contact person—maybe it's someone he met in prison—or he's being extraordinarily loyal."

"The district attorney's planning to talk to him again," Henry said. "Meanwhile, if this works and we catch the go-between, there will be no deals. They'll all go to jail for a long time."

"So how long do you think we'll have to wait for someone to take the bait?" Abby asked.

"With a buyer in hand, not long." He walked over to the couch, sat down and stretched out his legs. "Today and tomorrow I want it to be obvious that someone's in the house. The cars visible. Lights on."

"What about church tomorrow?" Mary asked.

"I'll get one of my men to come over and do some raking and trimming of the shrubbery in the front. The pattern for these break-ins has been on weekdays. I'm guessing Monday will be the most likely chance for our guy to strike. I want you both out of the house that day. My men will take over."

"I'll go in to the shop," Mary said.

"No problem for me. I'm behind in my work anyway."

"Make sure you don't tell anyone what we're doing, not even your parents or co-workers," Henry warned. "We have no idea who the contact is here on the island. If he gets wind of a trap, he won't show up and we may never know."

"Understood." Standing back, Abby studied the arrangement of artifacts in the cabinet. "What do think, Mary? Did I put them back in the right places?"

Mary smiled with a hint of nostalgia. "Jacob would be very pleased. Thank you."

"Don't forget to reset the alarm," Henry said.

"Oh right." Reaching to the back of the cabinet, Abby flipped the switch. Now they were ready for the go-between to make his move. She hoped.

AS MARY BACKED THE VAN out of the driveway Sunday morning, Abby waved to Deputy Mike Bennett, their designated undercover gardener for the morning. If the thief decided to steal the scrimshaw while everyone was at church, he'd thwart their efforts.

After church, the Stantons would vary their usual routine and come to Mary's house for Sunday supper. Mary had invited Henry as well as Mike to join them.

Along the picket fence bordering the driveway of Little Flock, red, pink and lavender rhododendrons provided a visual feast announcing the arrival of spring. Butterflies flitted among the blossoms, a powerful symbol of death and resurrection, of new beginnings.

Bobby, Abby realized, had intuitively sensed the importance of the pupae he'd discovered. In many ways, he was like those butterflies, darting from one new experience to another to discover all he could about the world in which he lived. She had no doubt that as a man, when he spread his wings, Bobby would be a beautiful person.

He was pretty neat as a kid right now. And later this afternoon, they'd release his small white cabbage butterflies.

Once parked and out of the van, Abby helped push Mary to the front of the church, Finnegan right beside her. Clusters of parishioners stood on the walkway visiting and enjoying the warmth of the morning sun.

Abby and Mary joined their parents and exchanged hugs and kisses.

"Did you hear about Frank Holloway?" George Stanton asked.

Abby shook her head. "No, did something happen to him?" Since Frank was nearly seventy years old, a health problem was always possible and Abby's first concern.

"He had chest pains in the night," her father said. "They rushed him the Medical Center."

"Was it a heart attack?" Mary asked.

"Thank goodness, no." Ellen put her hand over her own heart.

"Doctor Randolph decided it was only indigestion, or possibly gallstones. He'll have a sonogram tomorrow," George related.

"The news did give your father some second thoughts about the Men's Club's weekly donuts."

"Frank usually ate more than his share. They probably aren't good for him. Or me, for that matter." George didn't look at all happy about his admission.

Abby swallowed a smile. "Does that mean you're going to follow Dorthea Gilmore's orders and eliminate the donuts?"

"If we do skip the donuts—and I'm not saying we will—it will be the members of the Men's Club who decide, not some low-level civil servant telling us what to do."

"Of course." Hearing the prelude playing in the chapel, Abby took hold of Mary's wheelchair and pushed her to the wide open doorway. It wouldn't hurt any of them to reduce their intake of fat and sugar, but she was amused her father didn't want Dorthea Gilmore to have won the argument.

AFTER THEIR SUNDAY SUPPER, Henry elected to stay with Mary while Abby met Bobby and his family at the Nature Museum to release the butterflies.

Neil McDonald carried the terrarium out to the front of the building and set it on the low retaining wall around the bigleaf maple tree. Sunlight shifting through the branches speckled the museum visitors who had gathered around to watch the proceedings.

"Do you want to do the honors, Abby?" Neil asked.

"Oh no. This has been Bobby's project from the beginning. Let him do it."

They all moved back to give him and the butterflies room.

Squatting down, he eyed the insects. "What do I do? Just take off the screen?"

"Hopefully, they'll know enough to fly off when you do." Abby nodded to Bobby. "Go ahead."

"Okay." With a dramatic flourish, he removed the screen. "Fly away, fly away home!"

Nothing happened. The butterflies continued to sit quietly on their respective cabbage leaves.

"Try turning the terrarium on its side and gently sliding the leaves out," Abby suggested.

Carefully, Bobby followed her instructions. One by one, the butterflies and leaves glided out of the glass container. For a moment, the butterflies remained unmoving, and Abby feared the days of confinement had stifled their instinct to fly.

Then the smallest breeze wafted through the tree limbs and riffled the butterflies' wings. As though suddenly aware they were free at last, the butterflies lifted into the air. Wings fluttering, they circled above the onlookers as though saying good-bye. Then they each darted off in a different direction.

BY MONDAY MORNING, Abby's anxiety level about trapping the thief had risen to a high pitch. Her morning devotionals had done little to ease the stress and she was reluctant to leave the house. So was Mary.

"I wish we could stay here and see firsthand who else is involved in this terrible scheme and stealing our precious treasures," Mary said.

"I feel the same way." Abby pulled on a lightweight jacket to wear over her knit top. "But Artie's point about not becoming hostages is a good one."

"I know we have to do what Henry told us to. Still, I wish I could see the culprit for myself."

"We will. After he's arrested. Then the Seattle police will be able to raid Dominic's secret warehouse and recover all that stolen property."

"That will be such a relief for everyone."

Mary left in her van, and Abby followed in her car as far as town, then went on to the Nature Museum.

The whole drive to work Abby was on pins and needles waiting for this case to be resolved. The urge to sneak back home to be near the action was nearly irresistible.

As she pulled up to the museum, she forcefully reminded herself of God's Word: "The end of a matter is better than its beginning, and patience is better than pride" (Ecclesiastes 7:8). Henry would let her know the outcome of the case as soon as he knew.

AFTER LUNCH, Wilma Washburn popped into Abby's office.

"I just discovered the most interesting thing in the Family History Project report," she announced.

Abby looked up from her computer screen. "What is it?"

"Last week Hugo told us they caught Darren Barber in the act of stealing from Mary and arrested him for all the thefts, mine included. The name sounded familiar to me at the time, but I couldn't place him."

"And now you have?"

"Just now I was checking something in the Family History Project. There're hundreds of names. This may not mean a thing, but Darren Barber is about one quarter Salish, so he's listed in the report."

Abby wasn't sure that meant anything, except the young man might have an affinity for Native American artifacts—though he hardly seemed the type. Still, it might be the young man's motivation for stealing the antiquities, much as Abby had mistakenly believed Robb Phair was the culprit.

"And the thing is," Wilma went on, "that woman who's been harassing your father and the Men's Club about eating donuts?"

Abby frowned, not getting the connection. "You mean Dorthea Gilmore?" The woman who had apparently won the Great Donut War but did not know it yet.

"Yes, she's the one. She's Darren's maternal aunt."

Trying to absorb the implications of what she'd just heard, Abby stared at Wilma. Slowly, she said, "I dropped in on Tucker Billings unexpectedly Friday and caught him kissing Dorthea, which was a bit of a shock, I'll tell you that."

Wilma's dark eyes widened in surprise. "Tucker and Dorthea are dating each other?"

"Certainly seems like it. And now you're telling me that Dorthea and Darren, who we know is a thief, are related."

"Related by blood. That's a powerful connection among Native Americans. We're very loyal to our families. Even extended family members."

Abby got up from her chair to pace. She still couldn't believe Tucker was guilty of any wrongdoing. Unless Dorthea had somehow convinced him stealing items he insured was the *right* thing to do.

That made no sense.

But maybe Darren's refusal to confess and name his contacts was due to his loyalty to both his aunt and tribal connections.

She turned back to Wilma. "Do you suppose Dorthea gained access to Tucker's files and that's how Darren knew which homes to rob?"

"Tucker wouldn't let a stranger into his confidential files." Wilma's expression clouded over. "Would he?"

"Maybe if he trusted the woman and was falling in love with her. Or maybe he became careless about locking the files and she took advantage of his lapse, getting into the files on her own."

Wilma sat on the edge of Abby's desk. "Poor Tucker. Do you suppose he's been thinking with his heart instead of his head? He's never been married. He's not unattractive, but I can't remember him dating anyone seriously in years."

Thoughtfully, Abby removed her glasses and wiped them with a cloth. "Opal Collins' silver tea set was pawned in Olympia by a middle-aged woman with dark hair who used the name Mary Smith. Dorthea works for the state. She'd have a reason to visit the state capital for staff meetings or to see her boss."

"So you think she's behind the robberies?"

She was if Dorthea had a connection with Sylvester Dominic.

"I don't know," Abby admitted, "but I think I'd better talk to Henry. You may well have found the key to this whole puzzle. If he can get a picture of Dorthea, maybe that Olympia pawnbroker can ID her as the mysterious Mary Smith. That would connect her directly to Opal's robbery and it would be strong circumstantial evidence that she's a central player in the entire scheme."

When Wilma went back to her receptionist tasks, Abby placed a call to Henry. Granted, she had vowed to stay out of the investigation from this point, but the information she had now was too vital not to pass on to Henry.

She dialed the number. It took three rings before being answered.

"Sparrow Island Sheriff's Substation, Deputy Washburn speaking." The deputy spoke in a rush as though he was extra busy.

"Hi, Artie. This is Abby Stanton. Is Henry in?"

"I'm sorry, Dr. Stanton. We've got a mess down at the ferry landing. A whole bunch of cars piled up and one of them slid into the water. The sarge is down there trying to sort things out."

"I hope no one was hurt."

"No injuries reported. But I'm getting a slew of calls and the ferry can't depart, so it's going to be late getting to Friday Harbor. Sarge had to call Mike Bennett and all the off-duty deputies in to help."

Abby felt a moment of panic. "But I thought Mike was at Mary's house hoping the thief would show up."

"It's really a mess at the ferry terminal." In the background, another phone rang. "I can ask the sarge to call you when he gets a minute."

"Yes, please. Ask him to call my cell." She didn't dare leave Mary's house unguarded. Not when she thought Dorthea

Gilmore was behind the break-ins. And if Dorthea realized all the deputies were busy at the ferry terminal and no one was home at Mary's house, she'd know it was a perfect time to go after the scrimshaw collection.

Of course, Abby couldn't be positive about the woman without finding a direct link between Dorthea and Dominic.

First Abby called her father. Without telling him why she needed it, she asked him for Dorthea's phone number.

He found the number she wanted in his Rolodex. "What's this all about, Abby?"

"I'll let you know later. Thanks, Dad."

The next call she made was to Detective Costner's number in Seattle.

"Costner," he barked into the phone.

"Abby Stanton, Detective. I believe I've come across some information that may connect Sylvester Dominic to a woman who's been here on Sparrow Island off and on for the past month."

"Oh? What've you got?"

She explained the situation and then asked, "Have you tried to check calls Dominic made to Darren Barber?"

"Yep. Got his phone records here. There's no record I can find between Barber and Darren."

"Try checking this number." She repeated the cell phone number her father had given her for Dorthea.

There was a slight pause on Costner's end of the line while he checked the records. "Bingo! Dominic made a call to that number ten minutes after you and Hugo Baron left Antiques Galore."

"Then she's the go-between." Abby's heart rate accelerated

and she felt a surge of adrenaline. She'd connected the dots. Now someone had to stop Dorthea before she stole the scrimshaw and made it off the island.

"I'll call Sergeant Cobb," Costner said.

"I just tried. There's been a multicar accident at our ferry landing. He's all tied up trying to sort things out."

"I'll reach him one way or another. You sit tight, and one of us will get back to you."

Abby knew she couldn't do that. She knew Dorthea would strike this afternoon. The only thing that would stop Dorthea would be if she got to Mary's house and found someone at home. Clearly, she'd instructed Darren not to enter a house if there was any chance he'd get caught.

Dorthea certainly wouldn't risk being caught either.

All Abby had to do was get to the house before Dorthea showed up and make it obvious someone was at home. There'd be no risk in that.

If she could get there in time.

Cell phone in hand, she grabbed her purse and raced out the door to her car.

CHAPTER ❦ NINETEEN

MINUTES LATER ABBY turned onto Oceana Boulevard. From the corner she could see Mary's house. And a familiar car parked in the driveway.

Her heart lodged in her throat as she drew closer. It was Dorthea's car, the same one Abby had noticed disembarking from the ferry the day she and Henry had gone to Friday Harbor. Dorthea had beaten Abby to the house. She was, at this very moment, trying to steal the scrimshaw collection.

Abby pulled in behind Dorthea's car to block her escape. She had to think smart and fast. This was not the time to do anything stupid.

Grabbing her cell phone, she punched in Henry's cell number, a number she called only in a emergency. He answered after the second ring.

"Henry, it's Abby. Dorthea Gilmore's the connection between Dominic and Darren. She's at Mary's house right now. I'm here too."

"You're sure?"

"Absolutely. Detective Costner has the phone records tying Dorthea to Dominic."

"Don't do anything, Abby. Get away from the house. I'm on my way."

Henry disconnected. Abby looked up to see Dorthea coming from the back of the house carrying a heavy grocery sack. She wore dark slacks and jacket and heavy hiking boots.

Help me, Lord! Abby prayed.

Acting as casual as she could, Abby climbed out of her car. From inside the house, she heard the wail of the security alarm. "Oh, hi, Dorthea. Did you drop by to visit Mary?"

Startled, the woman came to an abrupt halt in front of her car. "She's not home."

"I'm sure she'll be along in a minute." Or, more likely, Henry and his deputies will show up. "Why don't you come on inside and I'll make you a cup of coffee or brew some tea while we wait."

"I don't have time. You'll have to move your car."

Abby strolled toward her, ignoring the still screeching siren in the background. "I'm glad you're here. I wanted to talk to you anyway. I'm so sorry that I interrupted things the other morning at Tucker's office. I had no idea—"

"I need to go now. Move your car."

"—that you and Tucker were seeing each other. He seems like such a nice man. Good looking too. Have you been dating long?" *How long will it take for Henry to get here?*

Dorthea turned red in the face. She stomped up to her car and tried to get to the door. Abby blocked her way.

"Get out of my way!" She used her elbow to push Abby aside.

Abby held her ground. "Perhaps you and Tucker can come over for dinner one night soon. Mary's a wonderful cook, you know. Far better than I am." Babbling was good. Killing time even better, if Dorthea didn't knock her flat.

Lowering her shoulder, Dorthea powered into Abby like a football running back.

Abby staggered but didn't go down. Anger flared in her midsection. "You aren't going anywhere except to jail." She'd taken some self-defense classes in New York at the local YWCA. Her skills might be rusty, but she thought she could gain control over Dorthea and hold her until help arrived.

Grabbing Dorthea's free arm, she twisted it behind the woman's back, much as Artie Washburn had done with Darren. She shoved her hard against the car. "Drop the scrimshaw, Dorthea."

"You're hurting me!" she screamed.

"Put the bag down now! Gently!"

She did as told. But instead of giving up, she reared her head back, bashing Abby hard in the face with the back of her head.

"Oww!" Pain exploded across Abby's face. Caught by surprise, her grip eased on Dorthea's wrist.

Twisting away, Dorthea yanked open her car door and grabbed for the grocery bag that was on the ground. Abby snatched it out of her reach.

"Give that to me! It's mine!"

"Not a chance," Abby said as Dorthea dived on top of her trying to get to the scrimshaw. Abby went down on her knees. Her face pulsed with pain. Dorthea was stronger than she looked.

Breathless, Abby used all her arm strength to shove Dorthea aside. Wild-eyed, she landed on the grass on her back. She grabbed a handful of Abby's hair and yanked.

Just then Abby heard a siren. *Thank You, Lord!*

"Give it up, Dorthea. The police are here."

Dorthea wrestled her way free and got to her feet. She started to run, but by that time Henry was standing right in front of her, his hand on his weapon.

"On your knees, Ms. Gilmore. You're under arrest."

Panting, Abby collapsed on the ground and sent up a prayer of gratitude that Henry had arrived in time. As she sat there breathing hard, she wiped her hand across her face.

That's when she realized she had a bloody nose.

TUESDAY NIGHT, Henry came to dinner. Mary and Abby sat at the dining room table in the soft glow of flickering candles while he brought them up-to-date with what had transpired in the past twenty-four hours.

"Dorthea was very quick to tell us the whole story," Henry said. "She's hoping a judge will go easy on her if she comes clean. She implicated both Darren Barber and Sylvester Dominic."

"Obviously, she has less loyalty to her relatives than Darren has," Abby commented.

"Not only that, turns out she was the mastermind of the whole scheme. Sparrow Island wasn't the first place in the state where she'd gotten to know an insurance agent who could inadvertently lead her to some valuable antiques." Leaning forward, Henry forked another bite of his apple turnover into his mouth. "*Hmm*, this is good. Cinnamon."

Smiling, Mary said, "I'm glad you like it."

"So poor Tucker isn't the first man Dorthea had seduced into unknowingly becoming her accomplice?" Abby asked.

"Right. She'd come across Dominic and his shady dealings and realized she could cut herself in for a share of the profits. Her job legitimately took her all around the state. She just had to find some poor suckers like Tucker and Darren to do her dirty work for her."

"But why?" Unable to fathom why anyone would want to steal another person's treasures, Abby shook her head. "She had a decent job. She couldn't have needed the money all that badly."

"Turns out she hated her job, and everybody knew it. She was pretty much walking a fine line and figured she'd be fired soon enough. So she was putting a little away for a rainy day."

"Or her early retirement fund," Mary commented.

Henry chuckled and slid his fork into the last bite of turnover.

"What about Dominic's secret warehouse?" Abby asked. "Did the Seattle police raid the place?"

He nodded, still chewing. "They went in early this morning and have spent most of the day taking inventory on what they found. They've identified Brenda Wilson's antique fishing rod, so she'll get that back. They didn't come up with her Salish water woman's mask though. Hopefully, they'll be able to track that down via Dominic's records and eventually recover the mask from the buyer."

"A buyer who'll be out a substantial amount of money for purchasing stolen property." Abby realized Wilma's mask could have been sold off as well and was glad they'd found it before it was permanently lost to a buyer they might never discover.

As Henry provided more details of the case, it appeared most of the Sparrow Island victims would get their property back. But not their stolen cash.

He pushed his empty plate away from him. "You remember there was a break-in on Lopez Island?"

Both Abby and Mary nodded.

"That was Dorthea's work too, not a copycat as I half suspected. She had to be over there checking on a state-run club for teenagers. The victim wasn't one of Tucker's clients at the time, but he had been before he switched insurance for cheaper coverage."

"So his records were still in Tucker's file?"

"You got it. The same for the estimate Candace got on her woven basket before deciding to decline the coverage. Poor Tucker feels absolutely terrible. I think he's going to help make up for the victims' financial losses when it's all sorted out."

"Sounds like all the loose ends are tied up." Abby stood to clear the dishes.

"Yep. After I left the ferry terminal yesterday, Al Minsky got his tow truck going and hauled that car out of the drink. Fortunately, no one was hurt, so the ferry's back on schedule."

"Then the only thing we have left to do this week," Mary said, "is go to the open mic night at Springhouse Café and watch Bobby perform."

"I'll go to cheer for Bobby,"—Abby gestured toward her face, where her nose was still puffy and she had two black eyes —"but I'll have to masquerade as a raccoon."

Both Mary and Henry tried and failed to stifle a laugh.

Abby didn't care. Dorthea was behind bars and the homes of her friends on Sparrow Island were safe from the threat of break-ins.

Thank You, Lord.

"There's another bit of news," Henry said.

"Oh, what's that?" Mary asked.

"Word has it that this morning the Men's Club voted to discontinue their morning donuts and substitute fruit and low-fat yogurt for their snacks. Seems one of the members had a heart attack scare and that decided the issue for them."

"That's so ironic," Abby commented. "Dorthea can chalk up one small victory for her diet police right at the moment her diet has switched to prison cuisine." She suspected the Men's Club's decision doomed Bobby's effort to get candy bars back into the school vending machines too. It looked like the residents of Sparrow Island were going to live a healthy lifestyle in spite of themselves.

THURSDAY NIGHTS were generally slow at Springhouse Café except during the busy summer tourist season. That wasn't the case for open mic night. The restaurant was packed.

Knowing it was sometimes awkward to maneuver her wheelchair through a crowd, Mary had made it a point to arrive early. She, Abby, Henry, Hugo and the McDonalds had taken a table near the temporary stage set up beneath a large picture window with a view of the harbor lights and the marina.

Finnegan settled down beside Mary, out of everyone's way.

The tables were set with the usual rose print tablecloths that complimented the deep green wallpaper with a similar rose pattern. The silverware and plates, which now held mostly scraps of uneaten food, echoed the rose theme.

Long before the start of the show, all the tables were filled and there were people standing in the back of the coffee shop.

She glanced around the table at her friends. Bobby had

barely touched his hamburger, and he'd been fidgeting since he'd arrived at the café.

"Are you all ready with your jokes, Bobby?" she asked.

"I rehearsed all afternoon. I'm ready." Worried, he glanced at his mother. "Aren't I?"

"Oh, honey." Sandy McDonald gave her son a one-arm hug. "You are so ready. Bring 'em on, I say."

Bobby grinned up at his mother, then turned to Mary. "Have you been rehearsing too?"

Mary gasped. "Absolutely not. I told you I'm not going to perform." Her hands actually began to sweat at the thought.

"But you made up some great jokes," Bobby insisted.

"And I intend them to remain our little secret," she said.

The others at the table started joshing her about her stage fright. She steadfastly refused to even consider telling a joke, any joke, in front of all these people.

"Well, Mr. Baron's gonna tell some knock-knock jokes, aren't you?" The boy looked hopefully toward Hugo.

"Oh no, I don't think I should do that, Master McDonald. I'll be rooting for you to win instead."

Bobby's normally smooth forehead pleated into a frown. "It's no fun to win if you don't have any competition."

Hugo leaned back and laughed. "Well said, young man."

"Then you'll tell some of your jokes?" Bobby asked hopefully.

"If you insist."

The boy gave Hugo a grin.

A portable keyboard had been brought in to provide some background music for the event, and the pianist struck a series of dramatic chords to announce the arrival of Cindy Kolfax, a young woman who'd been raised on Sparrow Island and now was doing the comedy club circuit. She'd been hired to act as MC for the evening.

She bounded out onto the makeshift stage, her astonishing carrot-red hair all short and spikey. "Hey, good evening, all!" She waved to the crowd. "It's great to be back home. The only problem is I forgot what the ferry schedule was." She held up a dripping wet swim suit. "Whew! I didn't remember how cold that water was either." She gave a vigorous shiver and everyone laughed.

She went into her shtick and had everyone laughing at her tales of being single in a world where men had all the power.

"Of course, that power only lasts till the guy gets married." She smiled sweetly. "Personally, I like the idea of a fifty-fifty marriage. My fifty percent is in charge of spending the money; his fifty percent is in charge of earning it."

Despite a couple good-natured boos from the men, everyone laughed.

"But tonight, ladies and gentlemen, is not about me. It's about our contestants who, I promise, are going to wow you. So let's give a warm Sparrow Island welcome to Brad Collins of Seattle. Come on up, Brad."

Everyone clapped as Candace's boyfriend hopped up from their table and strode confidently to the stage. Six feet tall with dark hair and gray eyes, he took the mic from Cindy.

"Hey, folks, I'm here to prove the rumor about attorneys isn't true. We do have a sense of humor."

He got a little chuckle from the audience and proceeded to tell a series of lawyer lightbulb jokes. Though at ease with a mic in his hand and comfortable in front of a crowd, Mary thought the jokes weren't much better when he told them than when Candace had.

He ended with, "You know, none of those lightbulb jokes are true. When we charge five hundred dollars for our services, we don't screw in lightbulbs. We hire somebody else to do that."

To the groans and good-natured catcalls from the crowd, Brad waved his thanks and returned to his table.

Margaret Blackstock was the next to take the stage. "Most of you know I'm the school secretary, and I gotta tell you," she said, emphasizing her Brooklyn accent, "you can make book on it. The kids at Sparrow Island Public School are the most creative kids in the world."

Everyone clapped at that, and someone whistled.

"They make up the most creative excuses for their absences I've ever seen." She waited for a few chuckles to settle down. "Take the sixth grader who claimed he was abducted by space aliens." She paused for effect. "Funny how those space aliens never show up on the weekend."

That got a good, solid laugh. On a roll, she related a few more excuses students had offered for their absences, none of them legitimate and all very funny. She got a nice round of applause for her performance.

Hugo was next up. With each increasingly awful knock-knock joke, he got a louder groan. Despite that, Abby had her face buried in her hands, her shoulders shaking with laughter. And she wasn't the only one amused by such a distinguished gentleman telling such dreadful jokes.

"Knock knock," he said yet again.

"Who's there?" the audience responded.

"Nobody."

"Nobody who?" they dutifully asked.

"Nobody. Aren't you glad I finally stopped telling knock-knock jokes?" With a bow to the audience, he handed the mic back to Cindy.

The audience cheered, relieved, Mary thought, that Hugo had knocked out his last joke for the evening.

A young man from off-island, who claimed to be Harry Houdini's long-lost thirty-second cousin Barry Houdini, performed an hysterical routine involving sleight of hand with cards along with his funny patter. The audience loved it. Mary laughed so hard, tears came to her eyes. Barry received a rollicking standing ovation.

After several other performers did their routines, it was finally Bobby's turn on stage. Mary so hoped he'd do well.

"I sure hope I never get my mother for a teacher." He sent a cute smile in Sandy's direction. "She's really tough. She'd never believe my dog ate my homework." He paused before the punch line. "We don't have a dog."

He waited for the laughter to die down before starting his next joke.

"Girls are all right, I guess. But I'm sure glad I'm not one. If I was a girl, I'd have to wear frilly dresses and learn how to curtsey." He did an awkward imitation of a girlish curtsey. "If I was a girl, I couldn't go behind the bushes to—"

"Bobby! Don't you dare say that word," his mother admonished him, and the audience loudly laughed.

This time his smile was less than innocent. "—dig up worms for fishing."

"Worst of all," he continued when the laughter quieted. "If I was a girl, someday I'd have to kiss a boy. *Ewww!*" He made a dreadful face to demonstrate just what he thought of that.

With each joke he told, he got more laughter until the audience was howling at his joke about how the girls chased the boys into the restroom during recess.

When he finished his routine, he got a rousing applause. Mary noticed Sandy and Neil McDonald could not have looked more proud if their son had just been elected president of the United States.

"Okay, folks," Cindy said, mic in hand again. "That's going to be a hard act to follow, but who wants to give it a try?"

Not a single hand went up.

"Mary, you gotta tell one of your jokes," Bobby said in a stage whisper everyone could hear.

She quickly shook her head.

"Come on, Mary. Your jokes are funny," he insisted.

Again, she shook her head.

Cindy came down off the stage. "Looks like we've got a shy comedienne on our hands, ladies and gentlemen. How 'bout we give her some encouragement."

All around Mary, people began to clap and cajole her to tell a joke. Embarrassed, she tried to wave them off. They simply wouldn't quit.

"Oh, all right! *One* joke. That's it. And you'd better laugh too."

Happy to accommodate her, Cindy handed Mary the mic. She didn't have to go anywhere near the stage.

She took a deep breath and exhaled. "We all know we're supposed to exercise. The truth is, since my accident I miss exercising the same way I feel about not having to clean a dirty house." She paused, letting them wait for the punch line. "I know it's something that should be done regularly, but I'd rather have someone else do it for me."

The crowd howled with laughter, including everyone at her table, which did nothing to slow the race of heat to Mary's cheeks. She handed the mic to Cindy and turned her attention to those sitting with her.

Laughing with everyone else, Bobby gave a big thumbs-up.

Cindy walked back to the stage. "I'd say Sparrow Island is home to a lot of funny people, but it's my job to pick tonight's winner. It's not easy, folks." She eyed each of the evening's performers. "First, for our runner-up and winner of a Springhouse Café voucher for a hamburger plate special—"

The keyboard player did an effective drumroll imitation.

Mary cringed, hoping Cindy wouldn't pick her out of sympathy for her physical handicap. Bobby should be—

"Bobby McDonald! Our youngest performer and a terrific standup comic!"

Bobby stood as everyone applauded their approval, Though he was obviously disappointed that he hadn't won first place, he managed a smile.

Cindy came off the stage with an envelope in hand. "Congratulations, Bobby. Enjoy your hamburger special."

Taking the envelope, Bobby said, "Thanks. I'll keep writing jokes so maybe next year I can be in first place."

Mary's eyes blurred with tears. She couldn't love Bobby more if he were her own flesh and blood. She was as proud of him as she could possibly be, not simply for his sense of humor and intelligence, but because God had given him a loving soul that would never be defeated.

To no one's surprise, the grand prize and voucher for brunch went to Barry Houdini. He hopped up onto the stage, and cracked a few more jokes that brought the house down once again.

As everyone started to leave, Barry came over to talk with Bobby.

"You were great, kid. Good going!"

"Thanks," the boy responded. "You were pretty good too."

"Yeah, I've been working at it a little longer than you have, but I still try to get all the mic time I can. That's why I came out here to Sparrow Island." He glanced at Sandy and Neil, then handed Bobby the brunch voucher. "Since I don't live around here, maybe you can use this easier than I can."

Bobby's eyes widened, and he looked up at his mother for approval. She nodded.

"Wow, thanks, Barry." He took the voucher. "But I'm still gonna try to beat you next year."

Everyone laughed, including Barry, but he didn't look too worried. Yet.

Later, on the way home in the van with Abby, Mary said, "With all the thievery that's happened in the past few weeks, I've been thinking that the culprits were stealing our treasures. But I'm having second thoughts about that."

"Oh? The scrimshaw collection was certainly Jacob's treasure."

"Only his treasure here on earth. The real treasure for all of us are the friends we have and our family, and the love of our Lord. The treasures we're storing up in heaven."

Abby softly echoed her own heartfelt *Amen*.

A NOTE FROM THE EDITORS

This original book was created by the Books and Inspirational Media Division of Guideposts, the world's leading inspirational publisher. Founded in 1945 by Dr. Norman Vincent Peale and Ruth Stafford Peale, Guideposts helps people from all walks of life achieve their maximum personal and spiritual potential. Guideposts is committed to communicating positive, faith-filled principles for people everywhere to use in successful daily living.

Our publications include award-winning magazines such as *Guideposts* and *Angels on Earth*, best-selling books, and outreach services that demonstrate what can happen when faith and positive thinking are applied in day-to-day life.

For more information, visit us at www.guideposts.com, call (800) 431-2344 or write Guideposts, PO Box 5815, Harlan, Iowa 51593.